JUST ABOUT PERFECT

Lori couldn't believe she was actually going out with Ed Beachley, who'd been the star of her daydreams ever since junior high.

"Hey, Lori, you look terrific," he said. And she knew she'd been right to let Hildy talk her into this wild new outfit.

It was still like one of her fantasies when they drove away in his copper-colored Camaro . . . until Ed pulled the car into a deserted lane and stopped. "Come on, baby, you know what I need," he whispered hoarsely. His mouth was hard and insistent; the kiss was going on much too long. And suddenly Lori knew that Ed wasn't exactly the guy she'd been dreaming about. . . .

FAKING IT

FIFTEEN #2

BETSY HAYNES

FAKING IT

A SIGNET VISTA BOOK
NEW AMERICAN LIBRARY

PUBLISHER'S NOTE

This novel is a work of fiction. Names, characters, places, and incidents either are the product of the author's imagination or are used fictitiously, and any resemblance to actual persons, living or dead, events, or locales is entirely coincidental.

NAL BOOKS ARE AVAILABLE AT QUANTITY DISCOUNTS WHEN USED TO PROMOTE PRODUCTS OR SERVICES. FOR INFORMATION PLEASE WRITE TO PREMIUM MARKETING DIVISION, NEW AMERICAN LIBRARY, 1633 BROADWAY, NEW YORK, NEW YORK 10019.

RL 4.5/IL 5+

SIGNET TRADEMARK REG. U.S. PAT. OFF. AND FOREIGN COUNTRIES
REGISTERED TRADEMARK—MARCA REGISTRADA
HECHO EN CHICAGO, U.S.A.

SIGNET, SIGNET CLASSIC, MENTOR, PLUME, MERIDIAN and NAL BOOKS are published by New American Library, 1633 Broadway, New York, New York 10019

First Printing, January, 1986

3   4   5   6   7   8   9

PRINTED IN THE UNITED STATES OF AMERICA

For Steve Jones and Ed Beachley,
a couple of gorgeous hunks

Chapter 1

Dumped. There was no other word for it. Lori Byrum knew she had been dumped. She had been in Boston visiting her grandmother for a mere two weeks during the Christmas holidays, and while she was gone, Monica Carrol, her one and only best friend since fourth grade, had dumped her to go steady with Steve Jones.

Monica had broken the news to her over the phone just minutes after Lori had started unpacking. "Lori, wait until I tell you what I got while you were gone!"

Lori had caught Monica's excitement. She could imagine her petite blond friend's eyes widening dramatically as she spoke. "Gosh, what?" Lori asked, envisioning a pair of front-row tickets for the upcoming Duran Duran concert in Denver or something equally fantastic.

There was a pause and Lori heard Monica sigh deeply into the phone. When she spoke again there was a dreamy quality to her voice.

"Steve Jones's class ring. Can you believe it, Lori? Steve Jones actually asked me to go steady."

Lori was too stunned to answer at first. Monica? Her best friend Monica? Going steady? Sure, Monica had had a monster crush on Steve Jones for at least a year. It was true that she had done a lot of nutty things to attract his attention, like the time she called him on the phone and pretended she was taking a survey for her sociology class on the personality traits boys like in a girl. But to think that Monica was actually going steady with him nearly blew Lori's mind.

Lori sighed, thinking of her own secret crush on Ed Beachley. What a dreamer *she* was. Ed Beachley was one of the cutest and most popular guys at Fairview High. So was Steve Jones. In fact, they were both part of the cool crowd, the good-looking kids with the great cars who always seemed to have everything. Lori remembered the long hours she and Monica had spent fantasizing about having Steve and Ed as their boyfriends, being seen with them, and knowing that half the girls in school were jealous.

"Well, I can't believe it," Monica continued, too excited to notice that Lori had not answered. "Of all the thing's I've tried to get Steve to notice me, something finally worked. And you wouldn't believe how nice he is. He's not just a hunk, you know?"

"That's great, Monnie." Lori finally found her voice, but the moment the words were out she realized that she hadn't called Monica by her nickname in years. Ever since the girls reached junior high Monica had preferred the more sophisticated sound of her full name.

If Monica noticed the slip, she didn't let on. "For the first two days you were gone I was totally climbing the walls. Then I got this great idea to go to the pool at the YMCA. I knew Steve worked there as a lifeguard, so I decided to go and take one more shot at attracting his attention."

Even though Monica had never been the shy, retiring type, Lori was a little surprised at her friend's aggressiveness. She tried to remember what Monica had done the last time she went away. For that matter, what had she done the last time Monica had gone away?

"So how *did* you get his attention?" asked Lori, trying to sound genuinely interested. "Fake drowning or something?"

Monica chuckled. "Well, I didn't go quite that far, but I did hang around his lifeguard chair and flirt with him a little. After all, you weren't there, and I didn't have anyone to talk to."

And I guess you couldn't stand a thing like that, Lori thought. The two girls had opposite personalities, which, according to Lori's father, was why they were such inseparable friends.

"Opposites attract," he would quip whenever the subject came up. "You complement each other instead of getting in each other's way." That had always been true. Monica was small and blond and Lori was tall with long dark hair. But their differences were more than just physical: Monica was the outgoing one, talkative and funny, while Lori preferred to stay in the background and egg her friend on.

At least, that's the way it had always been. Lori had always avoided attracting attention, claiming that it gave her stage fright. But she did enjoy the situations Monica's antics often got them into. Who knows? she thought. She probably would have enjoyed joining in a conversation with a handsome lifeguard without actually having to take any risks.

"So what happened?" Lori asked. "Did he toss you his class ring as he was diving into the water to save a drowning child? Or was it to show you his gratitude when you signed up for swimming lessons in the polliwog class he teaches?"

"No, silly. He asked me out for that night and every . . . single . . . night since, except for Christmas Eve and Christmas, of course. Then last night he asked me to go steady!"

"Wow, you must have really been spending a lot of time together," said Lori. She could feel her heart sinking into the pit of her stomach.

"Yes, we have," Monica answered softly. Lori knew what she was going to say next. "I guess he'll be taking up a lot of my time from now on. But I know you'll understand. We'll still be best friends and everything. You aren't mad at me, are you?"

"Of course I'm not mad at you. I think it's great," Lori lied. She was angry even though she knew she shouldn't be. It was great for Monica, but what about her? Hot tears flashed into her eyes. Don't be a baby, she scolded herself.

"Listen, Lori. I'll call you and we'll do something together," promised Monica.

"Why don't you come over now and help me finish unpacking?" asked Lori.

There was a pause. It lasted only a few seconds, but to Lori it seemed longer.

"Gee, I'm sorry, Lori. Steve's coming over in a few minutes," Monica said. Then she added hurriedly, "I didn't think you would get back so early. Honest. Well, I've got to go now. See you at school tomorrow. Bye."

Lori sat motionless, listening to the monotonous sound of the dial tone for a moment before hanging up the phone. She had been dumped, all right. Now what was she going to do?

The next day was a total disaster. Lori left home promising herself that she would make the best of the situation. After all, Monica Carrol wasn't the only living creature she knew, she reasoned. Actually there were several other girls she and Monica did things with from time to time. She and Monica. That was the hitch.

It had been the two of them who sat with Shana Beaumont at the home football games, laughing at the crazy new words Shana made up to the varsity cheers. And it had been Lori and Monica who had scooped the loop sometimes on Friday night with Pam Patterson. Pam was already sixteen and had her driver's license. There were others, too, like Angela Manetti. Her father owned Pisano's Pizza where most of the kids hung out. Angela slipped Monica and Lori free pizza sometimes and always refilled their Cokes without charging them. Then there was always mousy Ruth McDonald, but she wasn't much fun, Lori reflected. Ruth hardly said a word when she was around them.

In fact, there were a lot of kids who got together to see a movie or go for a burger, kids who just drifted into groups for an evening or two. But even though she was the one who made other friends so easily, Monica had liked it best when just the two of them did things together. She acted a little jealous sometimes when Lori seemed to be getting close to someone else. Lori hadn't minded, because after all, Monica was her best friend. But maybe I should have minded, Lori thought. Maybe it's been too easy for me with Monica always there, and I've gotten lazy.

Lori pushed her way through the crowded hallway, exchanging greetings with a lot of kids but still feeling very much alone. She sighed as she reached her locker and began working the combination lock. She had just swum through a sea of semifamiliar faces. So what?

A moment later she heard a familiar voice coming from just behind her left shoulder. "Hi. How was your Christmas vacation?"

Lori's spirits leaped. It was Shana Beaumont. Turning to answer Shana, Lori heard another voice coming from the opposite direction.

"Great!" Beth Schroeder called back. "How was yours?"

"Hi, Shana." The words were out of Lori's mouth before she could stop them. She felt warm all over. Shana would know she had misunderstood and thought she was talking to Lori.

"Oh hi, Lori," Shana said with a weak smile. She turned back to her conversation with Beth.

Lori yanked the lock and opened her locker door feeling strangely invisible. It was a new sensation.

She managed to get through first period without much trouble. Mrs. Manly kept the American literature class too busy with a reading assignment for them to be able to socialize. Next came Lori's study period, and she hurried to the crowded media center, dropping into the first vacant chair she saw.

"Oh, Lori. Will you do me a huge favor?"

Across the table, Candi Dawson was giving her a brilliant smile. Candi was head cheerleader for the junior varsity squad, and she had never asked a favor from Lori before.

Lori gladly returned the smile. "Sure. If I can."

"Will you trade seats with me? I have something really important to tell Kate." Kate Lund sat on Lori's left.

Sighing, Lori relinquished the chair to Candi. She could feel her face turning red as she scanned the room for another place to sit. She wouldn't sit down by Candi and Kate, even if she had to stand up all period.

There were vacant places at two tables near the back of the room. Lori headed toward one of them and then veered toward the other one when she saw that the first was occupied by Monica and Steve. They sat gazing romantically at each other. Monica looked up and saw her and waved furiously for her to join them, but

Lori pretended not to notice. Instead, she slid into a chair at a table full of total strangers. She didn't exactly know why she had ignored Monica's wave. Maybe she was still hurt and angry at Monica for dumping her. Or maybe she was jealous that Monica had a boyfriend and she didn't. Lori sighed for the twentieth time that day, thinking how complicated life had gotten in just the twenty-four hours since she had returned home from Christmas vacation.

For the rest of the day she felt rejected and ignored by every student in the entire school. By the time Lori reached home she was feeling desperate. She hurried into her room and slammed the door.

Sitting down at her dressing table, she stared at her own reflection in frustration. "What's wrong with me? Why doesn't anybody like me?"

Her answer was a loud purr, and Lori glanced toward her bed where her black cat was watching her intently with sparkling amber eyes.

"What do you think, Purr-vert?" she said, picking him up and snuggling him under her chin. Purr-vert arranged himself over her left shoulder and purred loudly. "You'd drown out a 747 on takeoff. Listen, Purr-vert, first I lost my best friend, and now hardly anyone else will talk to me. What am I? Washed up at age fifteen?" In spite of her misery, Lori giggled. "Washed up" sounded so dramatic.

If Purr-vert had an opinion, he kept it to himself. Lori stood in the middle of her bedroom, unaware of the red and black and silver stripes that had so recently replaced the pink-flowered wallpaper of her childhood. She stared absently out the window, stroking her cat.

"You know, Purr-vert," she said after a while, "I really do have a blah personality. I mean I always hang back and let Monica do all the talking—even when I have plenty to say. There may be a lot of kids out there who don't even know if my lips move. It's no wonder I couldn't get any conversations started today."

Moving over to her water bed, Lori gently placed Purr-vert on her spread and sat down beside him, rocking with the gentle waves. Pulling her junior high yearbook from the shelf of her bedside table, she opened it quickly to the individual pictures of last year's ninth-grade class. She was going to figure things out systematically.

"Jody Atterberry," she said, jabbing the photograph with a finger. "Popular! Why? Well, she was female athlete of the year last year. But she's also outgoing and nice to people." Lori scanned the next page until she found another name.

"Deb Bennett. Popular! Ninth-grade class president. Talkative.

"Candi Dawson. Popular! Captain of the junior varsity cheerleading squad. Never shuts her mouth.

"Hildy Franklin. Popular! Kooky and uninhibited." Lori fell back on her bed and stared at the ceiling as an idea began to take shape. "You know, Purr-vert, I'll bet half of them are faking it. That's it. Well, so can I! There's no reason why I can't be as popular as any of them if I put my mind to it. I've just been lazy in the past.

Sure, I could fade into Shana Beaumont's crowd, but Shana is loud and sometimes totally obnoxious. She really turns guys off. Or I could go around with Pam Patterson and her friends, but Pam only wants to drive around with her radio turned up full blast and wave to guys in other cars. Angela is okay, except she has to work at her dad's pizza place almost every evening. And Ruth? She boring, boring, boring! Okay, so none of them are in Monica'a category. But maybe . . . just maybe it's time for a real change. What do you think, Purr-vert?" Lori said excitedly, sitting back up again.

Purr-vert did not answer her with his usual purr. He was sound asleep.

"What did I tell you? If I put even you to sleep, I *must* be boring. Still," she told herself reasonably, "I can change if I really want to. I can become a new person. I know I can." She tapped her fingers softly on the smiling faces looking up at her from the open page. "And as this new person, I can become so popular and attract such interesting friends that Monica Carrol will turn a jealous shade of green." Lori nodded her head with satisfaction and added softly, "and all it is going to take is a little strategy."

Chapter 2

Lori closed her yearbook and gazed out into space. Suddenly her cozy surroundings faded and she saw herself standing in Schiller Memorial Field House. Gone were the bright wallpaper and red shag carpeting. Instead, she pictured row after row of bleachers climbing the gymnasium walls, filled with screaming fans. Beneath her sneakered feet the hard surface of the basketball court was polished to a brilliant shine. Lori's right toe found the free-throw line, and a hush of anticipation fell over the crowd. Wiping her sweaty palms on her shorts, she waited for the referee to toss her the ball.

"Steady, Lori. You can make it. I know you can."

Those reasurring words had come from team captain Jody Atterberry who was standing to Lori's right, arms poised for the rebound.

Lori shot her a grateful smile and glanced at her other teammates, who were looking at her with a mixture of hope and confidence. So what if the championship game was tied and there were only three seconds left on the clock? If she made these two free throws, it would take a miracle for the other team to score before the buzzer.

Of course she could make the shots. After all, Jody believed in her, and Jody was really someone special. She was such a fabulous athlete that the rest of the kids at school called her Ms. Jock, but that was only one reason she was so popular. Jody pushed herself to excel at everything she did and encouraged everyone else to make an effort. That's why it was so great that she was Lori's best friend.

The ref shot the ball into Lori's outstretched hands and blew his whistle. She bounced the ball a couple of times, concentrating hard. Then Lori let the ball fly. Whoosh! It dropped through the basket without even grazing the rim. The crowd was on its feet again, shouting her name and stamping. One more, she told herself. That's all it takes.

She took a deep breath and exhaled slowly as the referee passed her the ball for the second shot. She bounced it hard, aimed, and let go. The ball whispered through the net—a perfect basket. There was commotion under the net as the other team grabbed the ball and tried desperately to move down the court for one last shot. Then the buzzer sounded, ending the game.

A dozen hands reached for her, and Lori felt herself being lifted onto the shoulders of Jody and her cocaptain Jessica Mills, for a triumphant ride to the locker room.

"LORI! LORI! LORI!" chanted the ecstatic crowd. "LORI! LORI! LORI!"

"Lori. Lori." A single voice penetrated her daydream. Her younger brother Stan, a lowly seventh-grader, was calling her from outside her bedroom door. "Lori, are you asleep? Come on. Dinner's ready."

Lori was reluctant to let go of her dream, but at the same time she felt it slip away. It was just like that midget Stan to interrupt her. Why couldn't he have waited a couple of minutes? She wanted to see if Monica was watching from the stands and to hear the praise of her team-mates in the locker room. Especially Jody's praise.

Who on earth am I kidding? she thought. I couldn't make the basketball team in a million years. In fact, I've always hated the game.

"Lori? Are you there?" Stan called impatiently.

She made a face at the door. "Go back to your cage, already. I'm coming!"

Lori waited until she heard Stan stomp back down the stairs before she opened her door. She sniffed the air, hoping to catch the scent of some exotic new dish. She crossed her fingers for luck. If only it would be something out of *The Illustrated Step-by-Step Gourmet Cookbook*, her Christmas present to her father.

No such luck. She sighed and wrinkled her nose, muttering, "If this is Monday, it must be goulash."

Lori had long been certain that the Byrum household was the most unusual in Cedarhurst, if not in America. For one thing, her father stayed home and did most of the cooking while her mother went out to work at Serendipity Tours, the travel agency she owned, spent long hours at her job, and had to make business trips frequently.

Actually, Stanley Byrum, Jr., as her father signed his business correspondence, was a financial consultant. Although his office had once been confined to the guest bedroom, it had long since spilled out and engulfed the game room with computer terminals, printers, filing cabinets, and six telephone lines. He used all this neatly organized equipment to keep track of the stock market and other financial funds, the precious metals market, and grain futures. Then Mr. Byrum advised his clients on which investments to make and how best to increase profits.

Mr. Byrum impressed everyone with his efficient orderliness and total organization. It carried over to his shopping and cooking schedule. If this was Monday, dinner was goulash. Tuesday was pot roast. Wednesday, pork chops. Thursday, beef stew. And Friday—thank goodness for Friday—was always hamburgers. No one in the Byrum family ever consulted a calendar during the week unless they had a bad cold with a stuffed-up nose.

"Hey, Number Three. Will you pour me some milk, too?" Lori shouted to her brother. He was about to put the milk carton into the refrigerator after filling his own glass to the rim.

"I'm not Number Three. My name is Stan. Dad, will you make her stop calling me Number Three? It's totally gross."

"You are too Number Three," Lori taunted. "You're Stanley Byrum the Third, Number Three. While I, my dear little brother, am Lori Byrum the First—and only—Number One!"

Lori smiled smugly as she sat down at her place at the table. Calling Stan Number Three always made him mad, so she felt she was getting even with him, at least a little bit, for interrupting her daydream.

"Your mother called a little while ago," said Mr. Byrum. He was speaking in the slow, deliberate tone he used when he was trying to stop them from fighting. "She's going to be late. She has a client at her desk who wants to go hot-air ballooning and he wants to leave tomorrow."

"Hot-air ballooning in January?" questioned Lori. Then she chuckled and added, "Only Hildy Franklin would do something that nutty. It must be her father."

"The gentleman wants to go ballooning in Australia," Mr. Byrum said dryly.

"Oh, I get it," said Lori. "It's summer in the southern hemisphere. Megabucks. Hmm, in that case, it must not be Hildy's father."

Lori took a mouthful of goulash and thought about her kooky classmate. Hildy had come back from Christmas vacation looking like a punk rocker with her beautiful red hair cut short and spiked. She had worn high-heeled shoes covered with rhinestones, fuchsia cropped-leg jeans, and a matching shirt with the words: "Kiss me, I'm a Sagittarius" written across the back. As usual, she attracted a crowd of admirers as she bopped through the halls shouting to anyone who would listen about her plan to crash the Duran Duran concert next month and go straight back to their dressing rooms at intermission and introduce herself. Nobody doubted that she would do it. Hildy Franklin would try anything once, and Lori had often watched her with admiration from afar.

Lori's eyes clouded, and she saw herself standing outside the McNichols Sports Arena where the marquee flashed DURAN DURAN CONCERT TONIGHT! She looked around eagerly. Hildy would be here any minute.

Shivering from the cold, Lori reached into her pocket and drew out the letter that had come a day earlier. The English postmark had drawn her attention immediately, and as she opened it she had wondered who on earth could be writing her from England. The message inside was brief:

Dear Lori:
I have only recently discovered that I have a fabulous and beautiful American cousin. You! We will be giving a concert in Denver next week and I'm dying to meet you and introduce you to the rest of the guys. Here are two front-row tickets for you and a friend.

Love,
Simon Le Bon

Of course there were lots of people she could have invited to go to the concert with her and meet her famous cousin. But Lori knew that of all her friends, it would mean more to Hildy than to anyone else.

"Lori! Lori Byrum! Here I am!"

Looking around at the sound of her name, Lori saw Hildy pushing her way through the crowd that had gathered outside the sports arena. Dressed in a black leather miniskirt, red hose, and black high-heeled boots, Hildy looked more suited to be on stage than in the audience.

"Hi, Hildy. Isn't this exciting? Maybe we'll even get to go out with Simon after the concert," said Lori as they lined up to go inside.

Hildy had a dreamy look in her eyes. "With Simon ... and Andy ... and Roger ... and Nick. Oh, Lori, I'm so glad you're my best friend!"

The line seemed to take forever to move through the doors, and when Lori handed the tickets to the usher, he stopped abruptly and looked at her sharply.

"Are you Lori Byrum?" he demanded.

Startled, Lori fumbled for an answer. "Well ... yes. Is something wrong?"

"Of course not." The young man was smiling now. "Simon Le Bon wants you and your friend escorted to his dressing room. He wants to meet both of you before the show. Follow me."

Lori's legs felt like pudding as she hurried along behind the usher with Hildy beside her.

"This is the most fabulous night of my life," whispered Hildy. "And, Lori, it's all thanks to you!"

They were making their way along a corridor behind the stage area. Suddenly the usher stopped and gestured toward a door with a large gold star painted on it.

"This is Mr. Le Bon's dressing room," he said. "He wants to see you immediately."

Lori's heart was pounding as she reached for the doorknob. Wouldn't Monica die when she heard about Lori's cousin? She hesitated, then turned the knob.

"Lori! For gosh sake! Are you going to take all night?"

It wasn't Hildy, but the voice sounded familiar. Shaking away the cobwebs, Lori looked up into the face of Stan. Backstage at the Duran Duran concert had vanished and she was at the kitchen table, a cold plate of goulash before her.

"How dare you disturb me, Number Three!" Lori shrieked. She couldn't believe that he'd ruined another daydream.

"It's my night to do dishes. That's how I dare. I can't wait all night for you to come out of your trance." Stan glared at her as he added, "And I'm warning you. Stop calling me Number Three, or I'll punch your lights out!"

Lori pushed aside her plate. She wasn't hungry now. She was on her way back to her room when the phone rang. She considered answering it but decided against it. It wouldn't be for her, now that Monica had dumped her.

Stan answered it instead. "Hello." There was a pause. "Yeah, she's here. It's for you, Lori."

Surprised, she took the receiver. "Hello?"

"Lori, it's me, Monica." Lori's heart skipped a

beat. Monica was actually calling her. But why? she wondered. Had she broken up with Steve?

"Oh, hi, Monica. What's up?"

"I just had to call you. I just had to tell some-one, and you're my best friend. Lori, Steve is so wonderful. I really am in love. I don't know how I survived before I started going with Steve. And he loves me, too. He told me so last night."

Lori cleared her throat before she answered. The lump that was forming was so big she wasn't sure she would be able to talk around it. "Con-gratulations, Monica," she said at last. "That's great. I'm really happy for you."

"I knew you would be. After all, what are best friends for? I feel so much better now that I'm talking about it. I've just been dying to say the words out loud. 'I love Steve Jones, and he loves me!' Actually, I can't *talk* about anything else but Steve or *think* about anything else but Steve and being with him. Paying attention in class is absolutely the pits. Well, listen, Lori, I have to go now. We'll get together really soon. I promise."

"Sure, Monica. See you around. Bye." Lori started to hang up the receiver when she heard Monica calling her name.

"Lori, listen," she was saying as Lori put the phone back to her ear. "I'll bet Steve could fix you up with someone and we could double-date. Why don't I ask him? Maybe we could go out this weekend."

"Thanks, Monica, but I already have plans," she lied. "Bye," she added quickly, and hung up before Monica could respond.

It hurt to know that Monica was spending all

of her time with Steve just the way they used to spend all of their time together. Lori knew she should be grateful that Monica wanted to double-date; instead, she felt like screaming with rage. She didn't want or need Monica's help with her social life. She wanted to do it herself.

Her daydreams had been so wonderful, but could she ever make them come true? She was totally inept when it came to basketball, and there was no way in the world that she could come up with the tickets for the Duran Duran concert—much less a letter from Simon Le Bon.

When Lori got back up to her room, she found Purr-vert on the bed. Opening his eyes to golden slits, he observed her for a moment, then slowly uncurled himself, stretching from the tips of his ears to the end of his tail. He hurried to her, purring loudly, and Lori gathered him into her arms. She could never stay depressed long when Purr-vert was around.

"Purr-vert," she said with a laugh, "you are an excellent judge of character. If you think I'm so great, it must be true. How can I lose? It's back to the drawing board. I'll show all of them a thing or two!"

Once more, Lori pored over the pictures in her yearbook. "I'm choosing my victims," she informed her pet with a devilish gleam in her eye. It really wasn't a difficult decision. Jody Atterberry and Hildy Franklin. So what if they were two of the most popular sophomore girls in school. She'd just have to go for it, and faking it was one way to do it. She didn't have to be a jock or a punk. She could pretend. I even have a class with each one of them, she thought. It's going to be a piece of cake.

Rubbing her hands together in anticipation, she looked at the two smiling faces in the pictures and announced in her best Dracula accent, "You shall . . . become . . . my friends!"

Chapter 3

Lori's first big chance came as room 307 was beginning to fill for third-period history class. It was her most boring class, and ordinarily she hung around in the hall until it was almost time for the bell. But today she had gotten there early and had taken a seat by the window.

"Hi, Lori. Is this seat saved for anyone?"

Lori looked up, surprised to see Jody sliding into the desk next to hers. Jody was wearing a fantastic pink sweat suit that set off her short blond hair and peachy complexion. She looked as if she had just posed for a poster of the all-American girl.

This was it. Lori took a deep breath and smiled before she spoke. "Oh, hi, Jody. No, it's not saved."

So far so good.

Jody was smiling back, and Lori suddenly realized that she was waiting for her to say something else. Instantly Lori's mind went blank. Her heart began to race as she sat there looking

straight at Jody with the smile fixed on her face.
She had never had a regular conversation with
the star athlete before, probably because they'd
had so little in common. At least up until now,
Lori reminded herself. But her mind still re-
fused to come up with a topic for conversation.

What on earth could they talk about? She had
already ruled out joining the girls' basketball
team. The weather? The history assignment?
Lori couldn't even remember what the history
assignment had been. And even worse, she
couldn't think of a single intelligent thing to say
about *anything*. Here was her big chance, and
she was blowing it.

"Well, thanks," Jody said, shrugging. She
turned to say something to the boy at the desk
on the other side of her.

"So what do you think of Mary Lou Retton?"
Lori blurted out, regretting the words instantly.
But Jody was already deep in conversation, and
if she heard the question, she didn't acknowl-
edge it.

Lori slowly let out her breath, feeling a blush
spread over her face as two or three other students shot her puzzled glances. Why on earth
had she said such a dumb thing? Just being a
jock didn't make Jody an automatic expert on
all the Olympic athletes. Besides, the Olympics
had been over for quite some time now. Maybe
Jody thought that Mary Lou Retton was totally
passé, and that was why she hadn't answered
Lori's question.

I'm getting paranoid, Lori thought. Jody's not
a snob. Just the opposite. Strategy, she reminded

herself with renewed determination. I've just simply got to work on strategy.

At lunchtime Lori spotted Tripp Lefcoe sitting alone in the cafeteria. Tripp was one of the easiest people in the world to talk to. In fact, she felt almost as comfortable around him as she did around Monica. Tripp was a sophomore, too, but he seemed older, and somehow more mature. He was comfortable talking about things that were really interesting to Lori, things that mattered like the pressure on kids in high school to make top grades and get into a good college, different places in the world that would be fun to visit—good stuff like that—instead of the usual school gossip. Tripp was the sophomore editor of *Prisms*, the school's literary magazine, and someday Lori planned to show him some of the poetry she had written when her emotions were too special to express in any other way. But not now. She had other things to ask Tripp during this lunch hour, and she hurried toward his table so fast that some of her vegetable soup slopped out of the bowl and onto her tray.

Tripp saw her coming and grinned. "So where's the other Bobbsey twin?" he asked as she put her tray on the table and sat down across from him. "You and Monica on the fritz?"

Lori fought down the twinge of pain that the mention of Monica's name brought on. "Haven't you heard? She and Steve Jones are going steady."

"Come to think of it, I did see them strolling

down the hall gazing at each other and acting as if they were on another planet."

Lori felt her heart dive as an image of herself and Ed Beachley strolling through the halls crossed her mind. He would be telling her how great she looked, or they would be talking about places to go on their next date. Lori half smiled. She could almost hear the conversation. Suddenly she remembered the reason she was sitting with Tripp.

"Tell me about sports."

Tripp looked astonished. "Sports! When did *you* suddenly get interested in sports?"

"Oh . . . recently," she said, trying her best to sound casual. Tripp knew a lot about sports. Tripp knew a lot about everything. She was convinced that she could find out anything she wanted from him.

"Well, just which sports have you *recently* gotten interested in? Water polo? Big-game hunting? Or could it be tiddledywinks?" he teased, his eyes dancing.

Lori relaxed a little, grateful for his sense of humor. She started to reply that she was actually one of the best tiddledywinkers in Colorado, but quickly stopped herself. She was silent for a moment, thinking about how she and Tripp had always leveled with each other. She didn't want him to get the wrong impression about what she was doing.

"Actually," she began, knowing that it was the right thing to say, "since Monica started going with Steve, I've been trying to cultivate some new friends. And . . . well . . . Jody Atterberry is awfully friendly, and I like her a lot, but we don't have much in common. My strategy is to learn about sports—you know, sort of take a crash course—so we would have more to talk about."

"Smart woman," said Tripp. He raked his fingers through his dark wavy hair the way he always did when he was thinking. "Jody is captain of the girls' basketball team. Why don't you start going to the games? She's a terrific player, and we've won four of the five games we've played so far this season."

"Great idea," Lori said. "Why didn't I think of that?"

"You were too busy thinking up scintillating conversation. By the way, when are you going to show me some of this poetry you're always telling me about? The English teachers try to let us know which students could write for us. I've seen some of the stuff you've written for English comp, and if your poetry is half as good, I might be able to use some of it in *Prisms*."

Lori blushed with pleasure. "One of these days. I promise."

"Promises, promises," Tripp said, shaking his head. Their conversation turned to lighter subjects for the rest of the meal.

Lori was still thinking about basketball and Jody when she finished lunch and headed for the tray return. She wasn't paying any attention to who else was in line. So it was a total surprise when she heard Monica say, "Hi, Lori. How's your day going?"

Monica and Steve were just ahead of her, and

she felt a little angry as she looked at them together. She slid her tray onto the conveyor belt before she answered.

"Great! How about yours?"

"Oh, fine," said Monica. Then stepping away from Steve and pulling Lori with her, she whispered, "I saw you having lunch with Tripp. I know you two are good friends, but you seemed to be having such a serious conversation I wondered if it was more than just friendship. Have you two got something going?"

Lori tried to look mysterious. "I'll never tell," she whispered.

"Oh, come on, Lori. You can tell me. After all, I'm your best friend."

Lori looked at her coolly for a moment. "Don't be silly."

"I'm not being silly," Monica insisted. "I've always had the feeling that Tripp would like to be more than just friends with you. I've noticed the way he looks at you sometimes. It wouldn't surprise me if he asked you out one of these days."

Lori shrugged and turned to walk away just as Monica added, "Let me know if you two start going out, and we'll double-date."

Lori pretended not to hear. Honestly, romance was all Monica could think about! It was ridiculous to imagine that Tripp Lefcoe had a crush on her. It was true that he was good-looking, and lots of girls at Fairview envied her friendship with him. But only Monica would come up with the idea that Tripp planned to ask Lori out. Some friend, Lori thought. Monica's so hung up on Steve that she can't get together with me unless there are guys involved.

After talking with Monica, Lori felt more determined than ever to impress Jody Atterberry and Hildy Franklin and show Monica that she could get along without her—*and* without boys.

It wasn't until she was walking home from school that Lori realized there was a gigantic flaw in her strategy to make friends with Jody. This was Tuesday and the next basketball game was Friday night. Not only that, but what was so great about going to the basketball game and watching Jody play? Anybody could do that. Practically everybody did. It would be a compliment to Jody that Lori went to see her play a fantastic game, but it wouldn't really make an impression. It wouldn't convince Jody that she had a lot in common with Lori and that they should become best friends.

Lori kicked a rock out of her path and trudged toward home. She was back to square one. Maybe she should call Tripp later and see if he had any other ideas. No, she decided, it was her problem, and only she could come up with the appropriate strategy.

Reaching home, Lori dropped her books on the hall table and stuck her head into the game room. "Hi, Dad," she called.

He looked up from his computer terminal, flashed her a big grin, and said, "Hi there, sugarplum. How was your day?"

"Oh, it was okay," she said, trying to keep the dejection out of her voice. Then Mr. Byrum turned back to his computer, and Lori headed for the kitchen to see what was in the fridge. It was their usual routine.

But Lori stopped short as she noticed the stack of sports magazines beside her father's recliner. He was an absolute sports nut and pored over those magazines every spare moment. Then he and Number Three would go on and on at the dinner table about professional basketball and the NAB. Or was it the NBA?

Suddenly, Lori knew just what to do. She hated to disturb her father when he was working, but this was an emergency. Besides, it was almost time for him to put on the pot roast.

"Dad," she called softly.

"Hmm?"

"May I borrow some of your sports magazines?"

"Sure. Help yourself," he said. "Doing some sort of school project on sports?"

"Something like that. Thanks."

"Glad to help, anytime," he added absently, and Lori thought she heard him mutter something about what inflation was doing to pork bellies.

Lori felt relief as she picked up the stack of magazines and headed for her room. If Jody played high school basketball and was such a fabulous jock, she would have to be interested in professional ball, too. Everything she could ever want to know was in those magazines. Tomorrow she could make conversation with Jody Atterberry. Tomorrow she could impress the tube socks right off of Ms. Jock.

She started off by opening her notebook and writing Jody's name at the top of a blank page. Then she listed all the things she needed to know. Names of the teams. Standings. Star players. The list went on and on, and she wondered how she could ever learn so much in just one night. It was worse than cramming for a final exam.

Hours later Lori yawned and closed her notebook. She had it down. Her father had said she could eat in her room, and she felt a little guilty about letting him think she was doing schoolwork. But she knew it all. Larry Bird. Dr. J. The entire NBA. Now she could go to bed.

Then Lori remembered. Hildy! She hadn't seen Hildy today. Their gym class only met every other day. *Tomorrow.* The word sounded ominous. There was no way she could start a conversation with Hildy tomorrow without working out her strategy first. The disaster with Jody had taught her that.

Lori glanced wearily at her clock. Eleven-thirty, and her alarm would go off at six. She groaned and opened her notebook to a clean page. This business of making new friends was a lot more work than she had thought.

Chapter 4

The next morning Lori stood in her underwear with a towel wrapped around her wet hair surveying the contents of her closet. There were so many decisions to make.

"The problem is, what to wear," she told Purr-vert, who was rubbing figure eights around her ankles and purring noisily. "I could wear the new sweats I got for Christmas today and look athletic when I tell Jody how crazy I am about professional basketball, but that might turn off Hildy. She definitely isn't the athletic type. Or I could wear my hot-pink-and-orange striped mini-skirt and leg warmers for Hildy's benefit, except that Jody might take one look at me and throw up."

Purr-vert stopped purring and sat down, watching her with large golden eyes.

"Compromise, you say? With what?" Lori shrugged. She could always wear jeans, of course, and one of her nondescript sweaters. *Nondescript*. Ha! She was going to drop that word from her vocabulary.

"I'm never going to be nondescript again!" she declared vehemently, startling Purr-vert, who was now washing an invisible spot on one black paw. "It's simply a matter of timing. I could wear the miniskirt and get to history class and into my seat before Jody gets there and notices what I'm wearing. Or I could wear my sweats and get to gym class early and change into my gym suit before Hildy gets there and sees me. What do you think, Purr-vert?"

Purr-vert seemed to be thinking it over. Finally he raised his head and let out a long, plaintive meow.

"My opinion exactly," Lori said. "Hildy is always late, so I'll wear my sweats. I have a better chance of fooling her than Jody."

Growing excited about her plans for the day, she removed the towel, shook her hair loose, and reached for her blow dryer. Then an even better idea hit her. With a whoop, Lori picked up her cat, holding him high so that she looked straight into his velvety eyes. "Purr-vert. I've got it, and it's brilliant. Why didn't I think of it before? I have history class with Jody in the morning third period and gym class with Hildy in the afternoon fifth period. I could wear my sweats to school this morning and take my miniskirt along and change into it at lunchtime. Isn't that great? I mean, if I'm going to do this number on both of them, I'd better do it right!"

Without waiting for Purr-vert to answer, she dropped him back onto the floor and began drying her long dark hair. She feathered it away from her face in front and let the back fall in a smooth, straight line at her shoulders. This was going to be a great day. She felt like an actress. She had the lines and she had the wardrobe. Someday she would win an Academy Award and, in her speech, recall this day. At the very least, she would make two super new friends.

Wearing her new lavender sweats and carrying her miniskirt and leg warmers in her knapsack, Lori headed for school. She felt glorious. And the moment she stepped into the main corridor, she knew her strategy was going to work like a charm. She scarcely noticed lockers banging and kids tearing around, pushing and shoving and shouting to each other. All she could focus on was Jody Atterberry, tacking a sheet of paper to the main bulletin board beside the door to the school office. It was perfect. Fate. She wouldn't even have to wait until third period to go into action.

She hesitated for an instant. She had studied the NBA thoroughly, but she hadn't really planned exactly what she was going to say. "Slam dunks" and "alley oops" weren't the easiest terms to fit into everyday conversation. Maybe for openers she should just ask Jody if she thought the Lakers could beat the Oilers. It's now or never, she thought, and she plastered a bright smile on her face and headed for the bulletin board and Jody.

Jody's face lit up when she saw Lori coming. "Step right up!" she shouted, sounding like a carnival barker. "Step right up, Lori Byrum, and sign on the dotted line for the all-school ski trip to Vail this coming Saturday morning! The bus leaves the school at six A.M. and returns no later than seven P.M. It's sponsored by the Girls' Athletic Association, and we get a group rate on the lift tickets. It's going to be a fantastic day." Jody was smiling broadly and holding out a ball-point pen toward Lori.

Skiing! The word ricocheted around her brain. You've got to be kidding! Not skiing—basketball! she wanted to shout. Instead, she reached out and took the pen from Jody and heard herself say, "Wow! That sounds great." I'm having an out-of-body experience, Lori thought. She saw the hand with the pen in it actually sign her name on line two, just beneath Jody's name. She felt like she was watching the whole process from a distance.

"Terrific," said Jody. She was looking Lori straight in the eye, and Lori could see that she was genuinely interested. "I didn't realize that you were a skier, Lori. Do you ski much?"

"Uh . . . mmm . . . some," Lori lied, ignoring the fact that she had only been on skis once in her life when she was eight years old. She also ignored her vow never to get on skis again. "But I also watch a lot of professional basketball games on TV," she added, changing the subject. "It's awfully hard to make time for everything."

"Are you kidding?" Jody said with a laugh. "Pro basketball is a bore. The winners are always decided in the last five minutes of the game. College ball is much more interesting. Besides, with the play-offs, basketball goes on practically until summer." Jody's face lit up. "But the ski conditions in Vail are fantastic right now. Did you know that Riva Ridge has an eighty-five-inch base?"

"Gee, no. I didn't know that," said Lori. "Actually, I haven't been up yet this year." All of her prepping on the NBA had been for nothing—a pure waste of time. Now she would have to learn about college basketball—after she skied Riva Ridge. Lori felt as if she were digging herself into a gigantic hole, but she was powerless to do anything about it.

"In that case, ski with me Saturday. I go up every single weekend, and I'm dying to show someone what they've done at the top. You won't believe it. They've added a new expert slope that's tougher than the Jaws of Death."

"Tougher than the Jaws of Death, huh?" Lori could feel the bottom drop out of her stomach. "That's hard to believe, but it sounds great. I can't wait to try it."

Just then Jody spotted two varsity football players making their way up the crowded hallway. "Hey, guys!" she called. "Come on over and sign up for the ski trip. Lori and I promise to take you down the new expert slopes. Don't we, Lori?"

"All right, you two. You're on!" said Rod Springer as he grabbed for the pen in Jody's outstretched hand. Rod Springer, of all people! Lori's heart began pounding wildly. Craig Jordan was waiting to put his name on the sign-up sheet, too. He was smiling at her as if she were some gorgeous new girl in school that he had never before set eyes on. Rod and Craig were two of the biggest and most gorgeous football players in school. She and Jody were going to lead them down the expert slopes at Riva Ridge on Saturday? Impossible.

How did I get myself into this? Lori wondered as she fought down a rising tide of panic. Why on earth did I wear my sweats today and try to fool Jody into thinking I'm as much of a jock as she is? Why didn't I wear my miniskirt? Then she would have thought I was a rocker. Or at the very least, a wimp. Then I wouldn't be facing Jaws of Death. Or worse!

Like an answer to a prayer, the first bell rang. Lori waved good-bye to Jody and headed for her first-period class. This is only Wednesday, she reminded herself. Anything could happen between Wednesday and Saturday. A blizzard could hit the entire Midwest and the ski trip could be canceled. Or maybe a heat wave would come instead, melting all eighty-five inches of base at Riva Ridge. Or she could come down with bubonic plague or break both legs. There were all sorts of possibilities. Strategy. All it would take was a little strategy—and a lot of imagination.

Lori put aside thoughts of skiing for the rest of the morning and concentrated on Hildy Franklin. Hildy was going to be a lot harder to impress than Jody had been, but Lori had a plan. It was the most far-out plan that she could imagine, a pure stroke of genius, and it would take a lot of nerve to carry out. But it would be worth it if it convinced Hildy to become her friend.

When the noon bell rang, Lori scooted out of her class and hurried toward the girls' lavatory, stopping only long enough to retrieve her belongings from her locker. She had kept her fingers, her eyes, her ears, and her toes crossed all morning hoping she wouldn't run into Hildy while she was still wearing her sweats. She had been in luck. Now all she had to do was duck into a stall, change into her other clothes, and emerge with a look. Super rocker! she thought, inwardly pleased with herself.

Fortunately the girls' lavatory was deserted. Everyone had gone to the cafeteria for lunch. That was what she had counted on. It would give her plenty of time for her transformation. But as she yanked off her sweat shirt and began buttoning her pink blouse, Lori heard the outer door open followed by a shrill voice that she recognized immediately.

". . . and so I told that Ed Beachley that if he didn't get tickets for Duran Duran I would never go out with him again. I mean, really. A promise is a promise," Hildy said.

Hildy Franklin was talking about Ed Beachley. She had always made it known that she wanted to date a lot of different guys instead of going steady with one, and Lori had seen her with almost every popular boy in school. But why did she have to be dating Ed Beachley, of all people? Lori's stomach did a quick flip-flop as she fumbled with the buttons. Still, this was the moment she was waiting for, and she was only half dressed.

"But, Hildy, didn't you know that the tickets

for that concert sold out an hour after they went on sale? Most of the people who got them had been camped out in front of McNichols Sports Arena all night."

The second voice was Candi Dawson's. Lori stifled a groan. What was she doing with Hildy? She would only complicate things.

"So?" Hildy said in a pouty voice. "He should never have promised if he couldn't make good on it."

Lori hopped from one foot to the other, pulling off her sneakers and sweat pants. She had worn her orange leotards under her sweats and had roasted all morning. But it would be worthwhile. On went the hot-pink-and-orange miniskirt, the black leg warmers, and the black flats. Hurry! she thought frantically. Her hands were shaking as she dug into her handbag and pulled out a bright pink lip gloss, black mascara, and her hand mirror. Applying the gloss and mascara generously, she surveyed herself in the mirror. Almost, but not quite, she thought, and she spread a dot of lip gloss across each cheek to replace the blush she had forgotten to bring along. Finally. She was ready. But why had it gotten so quiet? Had she been concentrating so hard on her transformation that Hildy and Candi left without her knowing it?

Gingerly she peered through the crack in the stall door. They were still there, each intent on her image in the broad mirror over the sinks. Candi was brushing her long blond hair. With one hand Hildy was laboriously applying lipstick, the same shade of purple as her oversized jacket. With the other hand she was raking her short red hair into spikes.

Lori pulled a folded sheet of paper out of her purse and took a deep breath for luck. It was her only prop, and she had worked on it late into the night, writing with her left hand to disguise her own neat handwriting. Her big moment. She pulled the bolt, allowing the stall door to swing open, and stepped out.

Chapter 5

"Did I hear someone saying something about Duran Duran?" Lori asked, trying to sound totally innocent.

Hildy looked up from blotting her lips, surprise registering on her face. "Oh, hi, Lori. Yeah, I was just mentioning to Candi how that rat Ed Beachley was *supposed* to get tickets for the concert in Denver next month, but instead all he has are excuses. Hey, that's a neat miniskirt. Get it for Christmas?"

Lori tried not to let the mention of Ed Beachley bother her. She could think about that later. Also, she was determined to keep the conversation where she wanted it, so she ignored the question about her miniskirt. "That's too bad about the Duran Duran tickets. I can imagine how you must feel. Actually, I'll probably be going to the concert myself."

Hildy's eyes grew wide with surprise, and Candi stopped looking at herself in the mirror and turned toward Lori. "*You* are going to the Duran Duran concert?" asked Hildy. "How on earth did you get tickets? They're practically impossible to get."

Lori's heart was pounding wildly. It was working. Hildy Franklin was taking the bait—hook, line, and sinker. Now all I have to do is stay cool and stick to the plan, she thought. Then slowly and deliberately she drew the folded paper out of her handbag and held it out to Hildy. "I don't actually have them yet, but I'm sure that I will. Read this, if you don't believe me," she said in a bored voice.

Hildy grabbed the paper and began to read, her eyes growing even wider as she scanned the page. Her face broke into a gigantic smile.

"'Dear Lori,'" she read aloud. "'I have just landed a job mixing sound for Duran Duran's American tour. We'll be in Denver next month, and I was wondering if you would like to come down to McNichols Sports Arena and meet the group? I'll give you a call when I get to the city. Your cousin, Chris Byrum.' Lori! Is this real? Do you really have a cousin on Duran Duran's crew?"

"Let me see that letter," demanded Candi, grabbing it and gasping as she read the words. "Oh, my gosh!"

"Wow, is that ever great!" Hildy gushed as she moved closer to Lori. "It's really neat to be friends with someone who has connections to Duran Duran, isn't it, Candi?"

Candi was beaming one of her cheerleading

smiles at Lori. "You bet. I just think it's wonderful. Oh, Lori, you're sooo lucky!"

Lori reached for the letter and carefully folded it again before returning it to her handbag. "I know I can trust both of you to keep this a secret," she said slyly. "I know that a lot of kids would pretend to be my friends if they knew that Chris can get me as many tickets to the concert as I want." She paused, letting the words sink in before she spoke again, aware that Hildy and Candi were both nodding and staring at her with open mouths. "Gotta split. See you in gym class, Hildy."

Lori's feet barely touched the floor as she left the lavatory and headed toward the cafeteria for what remained of lunch period. She had left Hildy and Candi in total shock. When she had mentioned extra tickets, all they had been able to do was nod and watch her go. Of course, she would still have to figure out how to get out of actually producing the tickets when concert time came. She had nearly a month to work on her strategy for that. By then, she and Hildy would already be super friends.

She was still congratulating herself when she turned a corner and smacked right into Tripp Lefcoe.

"Oh, my gosh. Tripp. Where did you come from?" Lori sputtered.

"Lori? Is that you under all that makeup? Or are you masquerading as Madonna? Isn't that getup a little funky for you?"

Lori flushed, feeling suddenly foolish. She

hadn't thought about Tripp seeing her like this. True, she had worried about Jody, but that was different. How could she have been so stupid as to forget about Tripp?

"Hey, I'm sorry," said Tripp, tipping her chin so that she had to look at him. "I didn't mean that. Honest I didn't. It's just that you look so . . . different. That's all. The last time I saw you, you were about to become an expert on basketball," he went on. "I guess that's why it surprised me. No hard feelings. Okay?"

"So ask me a question about the NAB. I know a lot of useless things about it," she challenged. "Whoops! I mean the NBA." Lori giggled, then mugged for Tripp. "Or is it the BAN?"

Suddenly the tension was broken, and they were both laughing like crazy. "If that's the way you do your homework, I'm surprised you're still on the honor roll," Tripp bantered. "Do you spell any better than you initial?"

Just as their laughter began to subside, the bell rang ending lunch period. Lori said good-bye, feeling relieved that there was no time for explanations about the way she looked. She knew Tripp was puzzled, but she didn't want to tell him anything more than he already knew about her plans for making new friends. She wasn't really lying to anyone, of course. She was only faking them out. But even that would be hard to explain to someone like Tripp. He was so straight. He wouldn't understand what she was doing.

She had missed lunch altogether, and her empty stomach growled noisily through fourth-period Spanish class. What if I pass out from hunger during gym? she wondered, imagining herself lying spread-eagled on the basketball court, too weak to get up. She could see it all now. Twenty-five shorts-clad girls would be encircling her, and Hildy would be cradling Lori's head in her lap, trying to get her to swallow some warm chicken broth and murmuring, "Don't die, Lori. But if you do, may I have your Duran Duran tickets?"

The thought made her laugh out loud. Mrs. Hernandez, her Spanish teacher, frowned over the top of her glasses and shook her head menacingly. Lori turned back to the exercises in her workbook.

Lori stopped at the candy-bar machine on her way to fifth period. She devoured a Snickers bar to keep up her strength. Suddenly she saw two people farther down the hall. It was Monica and Steve, and they seemed to be arguing. Lori felt embarrassed, as though she were intruding on their privacy. She turned away quickly and headed into the gym.

The locker room was already crowded by the time she got there. As she waded through the crowd looking for a place to change into her gym suit, she heard a familiar voice calling her name.

"Lori! Over here. I've saved you a place," Hildy said.

She was bobbing up and down and frantically waving her bright green gym shorts over the heads of the girls between them. Lori's spirits soared.

"Wow. Thanks for saving me a place," she said. "This locker room's a zoo today."

"No problem," said Hildy, giving her a knowing wink. "Isn't that what friends are for?"

Lori smiled back at Hildy and extracted her badly wrinkled gym clothes from her knapsack. As she changed into them, she tried to think of something else to say. She couldn't let the conversation die right after Hildy had said they were friends. Still, she couldn't very well bring up Duran Duran or her imaginary cousin again since she had practically sworn Hildy to secrecy in the girls' lavatory. She wracked her brain for something else to talk about.

It was Hildy who kept the conversation going. "I'm dying to hear more about your cousin. You know, how many other rock bands he's worked for. If he's married. Stuff like that." She giggled. Then she suddenly got serious and whispered, "I mean, I know how awful it is to have a really exciting secret and how much it means to have one person you can trust. But of course, I'd never pry. You know that, don't you?"

"Oh, sure," Lori assured her. "I know I can trust you." But inside, she was panicking. She had just meant to use Duran Duran to get Hildy's attention. She hadn't meant for it to go much further. She couldn't back out now. Lori knew she would think of something. Strategy, she told herself. But for now, she had to act calmer than she felt. "We'll get together sometime, and I'll tell you all about it," she said.

Mercifully, Mrs. Crocker, the gym teacher, blew her whistle for class to start before Hildy could come up with any more ideas.

Chapter 6

Lori sniffed the air as she entered her own front door a couple of hours later and smiled. "If this is Wednesday, it must be pork chops," she said to no one in particular.

For once it was a relief to have a little predictability in her life. Nothing had gone the way she had expected. She had started out the day planning to impress Jody Atterberry with her knowledge of pro basketball. She had discovered that Jody was interested in college basketball. Then Lori had ended up signing up for a ski trip and promising to lead two of the best-looking hunks in school down the expert slopes.

Then there was Hildy Franklin. It had probably been a mistake to invent a cousin in Duran Duran's crew, because Hildy was going to bug the daylights out of her to get a ticket to the concert. Still, Lori reasoned, it was a lot more interesting than going around with Monica. All the two of them had ever done was sit around and talk about boys and occasionally go to a movie or out for a pizza. One thing was certain, though. There was no way she could change clothes again in the middle of the day. It was just too exhausting.

"Hi, sweet pea. Something wrong?"

"Oh, hi, Dad," Lori answered, trying not to let on that she'd been startled. "Nothing's wrong. Just sniffing the pork chops. They smell yummy."

She raced up the stairs and into her room before he could say anything more. She had too much to think about to get trapped in a parental conversation.

Purr-vert uncurled himself from his warm spot by her window and yawned deeply. "It looks like you've had a tough day," she chided. "Well, just wait until you hear about mine. On second thought, I'm not sure I want to talk about it."

She felt terribly tired. She had had a tough day, and her soft, warm water bed looked more than inviting. "I'll just take a short nap," she promised herself. She kicked off her shoes, gathered up Purr-vert, and stretched out across her bed.

She was awakened by a loud knock on her bedroom door. "Who is it?" she called in a groggy voice.

"It's me, Hildy. Can I come in? I've just got to talk to you."

Lori shot up so fast that she spilled Purr-vert onto the floor. Hildy Franklin! she thought. Here! What on earth could she want? Hildy only lived two blocks away, but she had never set foot in the Byrum house in her life. But

then, Hildy had never thought she might get to
see Duran Duran before, either.

She was wide-awake now, and she scrambled
over the foot of her bed and stared at herself in
her dresser mirror. Her clothes were a wrinkled
mess, and her face looked even worse. The bright
pink lipstick was smeared, and the black mascara had turned her eyes into dark sockets. Yuk!
she thought. How can I possibly let her see me
like this?

"Lori. Did you hear me?" Hildy called insis-
tently. "Your dad said you were in there. Or do
I have the wrong room?"

She was trapped. "Sure, I'm in here, and no,
you don't have the wrong room. Come on in,"
she called back.

Hildy swept into the room like a movie star,
smiling broadly. "I tried to catch you at your
locker after school, but I missed you," she said.
"I thought that since we lived so near each
other we could walk home together."

"That would have been great," Lori said, and
then her mind went totally blank. She smiled
uneasily. Here she was, tongue-tied again, just
the way she had been the morning Jody sat
down next to her in history class. It didn't help
that she had planned a strategy. The only topic
of conversation she had really worked on was
Duran Duran.

Now Hildy was beginning to look uneasy. "Listen, if you're busy I'll go on home. I just thought
it might be fun to get together and talk for a
while."

"I'm not busy," Lori said quickly. "I was just

trying to remember if we have any Coke or RC or anything. Would you like something to drink?"

"That's okay. I can't stay that long." Hildy sat down gingerly on the edge of Lori's bed and looked around the room. "Hey, I like your wallpaper. It's cool."

"Thanks," said Lori, and she was stuck again. She tried to think of something else to say about her wallpaper, but somehow she knew that telling Hildy that she had hung it herself would only make the conversation die.

"*Achoo!*" Hildy looked surprised and dabbed at her nose.

"*Gesundheit.* Are you catching a cold?"

"Gee, I don't think so. Say, who was that cute little kid coming in the door just after I got here? Is he your brother, or something?"

"Oh, that's just Number Three. Yes, he's my brother. What a pest."

"Number Three? Did I hear you right? Is he really named Number Three?"

Lori thought she would die of embarrassment. Why on earth hadn't she said his name was Stan instead of Number Three? Hildy would think she was some kind of nut.

"He's Stanley Byrum the Third, and I just call him Number Three because it bugs him," she admitted.

"Fantastic!" shouted Hildy. "I knew you and I were supposed to be friends. I'm a Sagittarius, and three is my lucky number. Isn't that great? *Achoo!*"

Lori's spirits rose. "*Gesundheit* again, and sure. That's really great." Then she added with a nervous laugh, "I'm glad he's not Number Four. One little brother is all I can handle!"

Purr-vert had been hiding under Lori's bed ever since Hildy entered the room. Now he walked ceremoniously out to the center of the floor, sat down, and gazed at her solemnly.

"That's why I'm sneezing," cried Hildy. "I'm allergic to cats."

Oh, no, thought Lori. What next? Scooping Purr-vert up with one hand, she tossed him into the hall and closed the door tightly. "Gosh, I'm sorry," she said. "I had no idea that you were allergic. I wouldn't have let him near you if I'd known."

Hildy was laughing again. "That's okay. Honest, especially now that I know you have a brother named Number Three. Besides, he's a beautiful cat. I've always wanted a cat, but unfortunately I can't have one." She paused again, with a thoughtful look on her face. "Actually there was something I wanted to ask you about," she said.

Here it comes, Lori thought. More questions about Duran Duran and the imaginary Chris Byrum. Then a new sense of panic hit her. Had Hildy said anything to Number Three? Anything about having a cousin who worked for the rock group? And what about her dad? He had told Hildy where to find her room. Had she asked him anything about Chris Byrum?

"Listen, Lori," Hildy was saying. "A bunch of us are going out TP-ing Friday night, and I wondered if you'd like to come along. We always have a riot."

Lori couldn't believe what she was hearing.

Hildy Franklin was actually inviting her to come along on one of her crazy escapades. Even if she was only buttering up Lori because of her cousin, so what? That meant her strategy was really working. It was too wonderful to be true.

"Sure. I'd love to."

"Great. We'll pick you up at seven, and then we'll head for the scene of the crime. And bring along some rolls of toilet paper. Scott or Charmin, if you have it. And make it pink if you can. Okay?"

"You're on!" said Lori. She could feel a new sense of daring rising in her, and it was all she could do to keep from jumping up and shouting.

"Well, I'd better scoot," Hildy said with a laugh. "And tell that cute little brother of yours that he's my lucky charm. Okay?"

Lori sat on the end of her bed for a long time after Hildy left, staring out into space and thinking about their conversation. It had seemed like a disaster when she found out that Hildy was allergic to cats, but then Number Three had saved the day, and now she had been invited to go out with Hildy and her friends TP-ing. Actually it was called lots of things. TP-ing. Wrapping. Rolling. Even Charmin Up a Home. And mostly it was done by a girl, with friends, who wanted to tell some guy how much she liked him. Lori sighed. She had forgotten to ask Hildy whose house they were going to roll. Oh, well, she thought. I guess it really doesn't matter.

The next two days flew by so quickly that Lori didn't have time to get nervous about the weekend. She rented ski equipment from the local sporting-goods store on Thursday after school and spent most of the evening trying on her boots and figuring out how the bindings worked. She was feeling better about her strategy, since Jody and Hildy kept starting conversations with her as if they had been friends for ages.

In history class, Jody couldn't stop talking to her about the ski trip. "So many kids have signed up that we might have to take a second bus. Isn't that great?" she had said excitedly, adding, "Even if we do have two buses, don't forget that you're sitting with me."

Then on Friday, Hildy made a big deal in front of everybody in gym class about having something really private to talk to Lori about and then taking her aside and saying, "Don't forget. Tonight's the big night. I'll pick you up at seven."

Lori had tried to act calm when she told her parents she was going to a movie with Hildy Franklin. She knew that it wasn't exactly the truth, but they wouldn't have let her go out if she'd said what she was really doing. She had even hidden two rolls of pink Charmin in a paper bag under the front bush when no one was looking.

A horn honked out front at seven o'clock on the dot. Lori's knees were shaking as she yelled good-bye and ran out to the car, hesitating only long enough to get the rolls from under the bush.

"Get in quick!" Hildy yelled from the driver's seat as Lori opened the door on the passenger's side.

"Hildy! What are you doing driving?" Lori shouted. In the backseat were Candi Dawson, Meg Stevens, and Trish Lowery, all Hildy's friends. Hildy was in the front seat alone, behind the steering wheel. "I thought one of your parents would be driving. How did you get the car? You're only fifteen. You don't have a driver's license!"

"Get in and be quiet," Candi Dawson called from the backseat.

"And hurry up," Hildy instructed. "If your parents hear you, it'll all be over."

Lori ducked into the car and closed the door as quietly as she could. Her heart was pounding. She hadn't counted on anything like this.

"You didn't answer me," she insisted as Hildy backed out of the driveway and headed out of the neighborhood. "What are you doing with the car?"

Hildy's face lit up and she began to laugh. "I borrowed it!" she sang. "My parents will never notice that it's gone. Like I told you before, they mostly doze in front of television at night. And besides, it won't be gone that long. It only takes a few minutes to TP a house. I'll have this car back safe and sound in the garage before they can change the channel on the TV set. Don't worry! Just leave everything to me."

Lori sank back against the seat. What had she gotten herself into?

Chapter 7

Trafalgar Court was bathed in white moonlight and as silent as a tomb. Hildy switched off the headlights and coasted to a stop across the street from a two-story Colonial house. At the end of the cul-de-sac, the house was set far back from the street, surrounded by leafless trees which spread eerie shadows across the lawn. The drapes were closed at all the windows, and only a soft glow lighted one of the downstairs rooms.

"Whose house is it?" Lori asked excitedly.

"Ed Beachley's. Who else?" said Hildy.

"Ed Beachley's?" Lori echoed in astonishment. She couldn't believe it. Ed Beachley, the boy of her dreams. She had known that he lived in this part of Cedarhurst, but to be in front of his house with her arms full of toilet paper and ready for the attack was almost too wonderful to be true.

"Sure," said Hildy. "Just because I'm mad at him over the Duran Duran tickets doesn't mean I don't still like him."

"If you change your mind and decide to dump him, I'll take him," piped up Meg from the backseat.

"Me, too," said Candi. "From what I hear, he's really one good kisser."

"I'll never tell," said Hildy, winking.

Lori felt herself blushing. She pulled her ski mask down so no one would notice. She couldn't stand to think of Ed kissing Hildy after all her own dreams about him.

Hildy pulled her ski mask down, too. They had agreed to wear dark clothing and masks just in case someone spotted them, but Lori felt a stab of apprehension.

"What if somebody looks out a window and sees us, dark clothes and all?"

"Don't be silly, Lori," said Trish. "Nobody stands around looking out their windows at night. Nobody is going to see us."

"And they won't be able to recognize us if they do," added Meg.

"Well, what if somebody comes out," Lori insisted. "People do go places at night, you know."

"Oh, brother," said Hildy, rolling her eyes in disgust. "It isn't as if we're blowing up a house or something. We're just wrapping it. Even if we get caught, it's no big deal. Are you chicken or what?"

Lori shot another glance at Ed's house. Hildy was right. It was just good clean fun, and she was going to be part of it. Besides, wasn't TP-ing a house a secret way of telling a boy that you liked him?

"Of course not. Come on. Let's do it!" Lori said, in the spirit of the adventure.

Carrying her two rolls of pink Charmin, Lori got out of the car and tiptoed across the street. Hildy was just ahead of her. "Over here," she whispered, motioning Lori and the others toward a clump of bushes. "We'll open up the rolls."

The five girls knelt on the frosty ground behind the bushes and began tearing the coverings off the toilet paper. A dog barked in the distance, but all remained quiet in the cul-de-sac. Lori scanned the other houses on the street for signs of life, but to her great relief they were all dark, too.

"I see you brought Charmin," said Meg, nodding toward Lori's rolls. "It's great. It sticks to the trees."

"I brought Scott," said Trish, giggling softly. "It doesn't stick as well as Charmin, but it has more sheets per roll so it goes farther."

"What matters most is that it's pink. That way he'll know we did it for love," said Hildy. Then turning to Lori she asked, "Have you ever done this before?"

"No," Lori admitted.

"Okay. So hold the roll like this," instructed Hildy, turning her palm up and placing a roll of Charmin in her hand. "Let out about twenty squares. They'll work like a tail on a kite. Then aim it toward the top of the trees. Be sure to throw underhanded, though. You'll get more distance that way."

Lori felt her heart pounding as she took a roll

in her hand just the way Hildy had shown her, unrolled twenty squares, and took aim.

"Okay," whispered Hildy. "You're ready with a little love message for Ed. Fire!"

Lori pulled back her arm, thinking how surprised Hildy would be if she knew that this particular love message was sincere. Then she looked toward the top of the tallest tree and pitched the roll, watching gleefully as it took off like a rocket leaving a contrail of fluttering paper in its wake.

"Bull's-eye!" hissed Candi as the roll vaulted upward and snagged in the branches. Then it bounced down from branch to branch, unrolling as it went along and getting skinnier and skinnier until only the inner tube fluttered down to the ground. "Right on target," Candi added.

The girls spread out across the yard, each armed with rolls of paper. Lori couldn't help smiling and thinking that they looked more like drunks staggering across the grass than teenage girls as they wove around trees and ducked in and out of shadows. She grabbed another roll and aimed for another tree. This was more fun than she had thought. If only she could be there when Ed came home and saw it. She could just imagine the look on his face.

Her aim was off, and she watched in horror as the toilet paper missed the treetop and landed on the roof with a thud. Instantly everyone heard it and froze, their eyes fastened on the front door. Lori had visions of Mr. Beachley storming out into the yard and demanding to know who was throwing things at his house. Seconds dragged by, but the door didn't open.

"I think we're safe," Hildy whispered loudly. "But just to be sure, let's cool it behind that bush for a couple of minutes." Then she motioned to the others to get out of sight.

Lori nodded and melted into the shadows. Hildy followed, and they sat in total silence for what seemed to be ages. With all sounds muffled by the ski mask, the only thing she could hear was her own breathing. Her breath rose into the air in frosty puffs like miniature ghosts taking flight.

An instant later Hildy was on her feet again. "Come on, Lori. Shoot another one."

Lori grabbed another roll and felt the excitement returning. She would make this one good, or else. It rose in the air and hung at the top of the loop for an instant like a roller coaster poised for the plunge, and then it came careening down through the branches, leaving wisps of paper on every one it touched. She clasped a hand over her mouth; she wanted to explode with excitement. Instead, she threw another and another.

Beside her, Hildy was gathering the remaining rolls, and then she motioned to Lori. "Let's go up close to the house. We'll wrap the bushes with what's left on the rolls. And for goodness sake, be quiet when you get near the windows. You'll get us all in for it." Hildy couldn't be serious either, and each time the girls looked at each other, they burst into another round of giggles.

When the last one had been thrown, Hildy and Candi raced across the lawn, scooping up the nearly empty rolls. Silently the girls crept toward the shrubbery lining the front of the house, carefully avoiding each other's looks so they wouldn't giggle all over again. They worked in silence, winding the pink paper in and out of the branches like garlands on a Christmas tree.

Suddenly Hildy held up one hand and frowned. "Listen," she whispered. "I hear a car coming."

Slowly the headlights of an automobile came into view, and the girls ducked behind the bushes. They watched as the lights slashed the darkness like twin sword points. The car was creeping along. It's only someone looking for an address, Lori reassured herself. But just then it passed under a streetlight, and she could see that it was a police patrol car moving down the street. It stopped in front of the Beachley house, and the officer who was driving gazed up at the draped branches.

Lori felt Hildy's hand close around her arm. "Stay down," Hildy whispered. "If they don't see us, they'll go on by. They never stop unless they actually see kids TP-ing a house."

The police car began to move again and turned out of sight around a corner. As soon as it was gone, Meg's head popped up above the bush where she was hiding. "Whew!" she whispered.

"Let's get out of here," urged Lori as she crept out of her hiding place on all fours. "The place looks great, and I don't want to take any more chances on getting caught."

"Oh, Lori. You're such a chicken. You really are," said Hildy in a disgruntled voice. "We've only got two more bushes to wrap, and we'll be finished. Besides, they went on by, didn't they? What reason would they have to come back?"

"I guess you're right," conceded Lori. "And I'll admit, I'd hate to leave. This place looks like a pink winter wonderland. If only I had thought to bring my camera."

The girls worked quickly, finishing the next bush in record time. They had just started on the last one when Lori perked up her ears.

"Uh-oh," she whispered. "I think I hear another car coming."

They all ducked again, falling behind the bushes just as the same police car pulled back into sight. It had apparently turned around and was heading into the cul-de-sac for the second time. Lori heard Hildy gasp as the patrol car pulled up to a stop behind her parents' dark sedan and a police officer got out and approached it.

"You'd better call this in," he yelled to his partner in the patrol car. "It's the same plate number and description as the one reported stolen."

Chapter 8

The static on the police radio crackled in the cold night air, and the voice of the second officer was clearly audible through the open interior of the patrol car. "This is Sergeant Ralph O'Donnell. My partner, Sergeant Logan, and I believe we have located the automobile reported missing from the seven-hundred block of Central Drive. It is a black, four-door sedan. Colorado license number seven-nine-two-six-six-zero-six. It's parked at the entrance to Buckingham Court, and there's no sign of a driver. Ten-four."

"Hildy! Did you hear that?" Lori whispered. "They think the car is stolen!"

Hildy was frowning. "Can you believe my parents? I mean, they are so square. You'd think that they would wait a little bit to see if it turned up or if I knew anything about it before they called the police," she growled. "But don't worry. All we have to do is explain the situation to those two cops, and everything will be okay. Come on. Let's go talk to them."

She started to stand up, but Lori grabbed her arm and pulled her back before her head rose above the bushes.

"Are you crazy? You don't have a driver's license, and we just finished TP-ing this house. Do you honestly think that they're going to laugh the whole thing off and go on about their business as if nothing had happened?"

Hildy shrugged. "Sure. Why not?" Shaking her arm loose from Lori's grasp and pulling off her ski mask, she stood up and marched toward the street. There was nothing Lori could do but follow Hildy and hope for the best. Silently, the other girls followed, taking off their ski masks as they walked. Lori could see from the expressions on their faces that they were just as apprehensive as she was.

"Hello, Officer," Hildy said to the policeman standing beside the car. "Is there something wrong?" She was wearing her wide-eyed innocent look, and Lori held her breath, praying that Sergeant Logan would fall for it. He was well over six feet tall with a beefy build and a square jaw, and he didn't look to her as if he took any nonsense from anybody.

"Yes, miss," responded the officer. He nodded respectfully to her and then to the other girls before he continued speaking. "This car has been reported stolen. Do you know anything about it?"

"Of course. It belongs to my father, Theodore F. Franklin of seven-eleven Central Drive. What on earth makes you think it's stolen? There must be some mistake."

"It was reported stolen, miss. I'd like to see your driver's license, please."

Here it comes, thought Lori, but Hildy ignored the officer's request to see her license. She went right on speaking at a breathless rate of speed.

"Daddy was sound asleep in front of the television set when it was time for me to go out this evening, and he was so tired and he looked so peaceful that I didn't want to disturb him, so I just went ahead and borrowed the car. I probably should have left him a note, but I didn't think of it, and I was sure he wouldn't mind anyway. Actually, I was on my way home right now. All I have to do is drop off my friends at their houses, and I'll go straight home," she said, flashing a brilliant smile.

"Miss, I'd like to see your driver's license. Please." He put extra emphasis on the word *please*, and Lori exchanged worried glances with Candi. She had the feeling that Hildy wasn't off the hook yet. Just then, the second officer, O'Donnell, climbed out of the car and joined them.

He looked sternly from one girl to the other and then, as if he hadn't overheard a word that had been said, he asked, "What's the trouble?" Scare tactics, Lori thought. He looked younger than the other policeman. His mouth was set in a line, but his eyes were friendly and concerned.

"Oh, Officer," Hildy gushed. "Maybe I can explain it all so that you can understand."

A smile twitched at the corner of Sergeant

O'Donnell's mouth. He seemed to be looking Hildy over approvingly. "Sure," he said.

She moved closer to him and began speaking in confidential tones. "Actually, the reason I didn't ask my father for the car was because I knew he would want to know where I was going. You see, my friend has a humongous crush on Ed Beachley, the boy who lives over there." She gestured toward Lori, and Lori's heart nearly stopped. Could Hildy possibly know how she felt about Ed? Of course not, she reasoned. Then Hildy pointed to the Beachley house with the toilet paper streaming from the trees, and went on talking. "The way to tell a guy that you like him is to TP his house, but my father is so straight that I knew he'd never let me help her do it. So I borrowed the car for a little while. That's all there is to it. Honest."

The young officer glanced toward the Beachley house and chuckled. Seeing him smile, Hildy moved a step closer and said encouragingly, "I'll bet girls TP your house all the time, Sergeant O'Donnell."

Sergeant Logan cleared his throat loudly. "I'll ask you one more time. May I see your driver's license?"

"I . . . I didn't bring my purse with me," Hildy stammered, and then she looked beseechingly at Sergeant O'Donnell and said, "I was afraid I'd lose it in the dark. You can understand that, can't you?"

"Of course," the sergeant assured her. Then he turned to his partner and said in an official-sounding voice, "I think we can clear this matter up pretty simply, Don. Just leave it to me."

Sergeant Logan shrugged as if to defer to Sergeant O'Donnell, but Lori could see that he wasn't pleased to do that. Still, she had to admit that she had a new admiration for Hildy. She not only had the nerve to try to talk her way out of this mess, she was getting away with it.

Sergeant O'Donnell did not give the other officer time to change his mind. "Miss," he said to Hildy, "you say you know the people who live in this house? Beachley? Was that the name you used?"

"That's right!" Hildy's face lit up. "At least we know their son. I doubt if he's home right now, though. You know, since it's Friday night, and most kids go out on Friday night."

Lori's heart sank. The last thing she wanted was to knock on Ed's door and announce that she was the one who had just TP-ed his house. Well, maybe not the very last thing, she conceded to herself. Going to jail for auto theft would definitely rank a little further down the list.

"Let's go talk to them," said Sergeant O'-Donnell, and he turned and walked briskly up the Beachleys' front walk and rang the bell. A moment later, an elderly gentleman with a balding head opened the door.

"Yes?" he said, squinting into the night. Then, seeing the police officer standing there, he looked startled and asked, "Officer! What is it? Is something wrong?"

"Don't be alarmed, sir. Are you Mr. Beachley?"

"Beachley?" the man said with a frown. "He lives the next court over. Over on Trafalgar. This is Buckingham. But they do look a lot alike in the dark. What the devil is that stuff hanging all over my trees?"

Lori groaned. Sergeant O'Donnell was shuffling his feet and looking embarrassed, and the other officer's face was red with anger, but Hildy suddenly exploded in a fit of laughter.

"You're kidding! You absolutely have to be kidding!" she shrieked. "Do you mean that after all of this, we got the wrong street and we TP-ed the wrong house?"

She was laughing so hard that Lori couldn't help smiling. It was pretty funny when you thought about it, she told herself. Suddenly she noticed that the elderly gentleman was smiling, too, and so were both of the police officers. That Hildy, she thought. She really knows how to handle things.

Hildy wiped tears off her face and made an effort to stop laughing, but every few seconds she burst out in a new fit of giggles. Finally she seemed to be in control, and she turned back to the man at the door. "I'm really sorry about the stuff in the trees," she said. "I don't know how it happened, but we honestly did get the wrong house. My friends and I will pull it all down just as soon as we can. I promise."

The man looked from Hildy to Lori and back again, and then his eyes began to twinkle. "Well now, I haven't had my house TP-ed since sometime way back last summer," he said matter-of-factly.

Lori's eyes grew wide as she looked at the man again. Do old ladies TP guys' houses, too? she wondered. Suddenly a picture sprang into her mind of two white-haired women dancing around the front yard in the dead of night pitching toilet paper into the trees, and she suppressed a smile.

"Of course, that was when my teenage grandson was spending a few weeks here," he said with a chuckle. He added to himself, "Beachley? Nice-looking boy, as I remember."

No one said anything for a moment, and Lori was beginning to feel uneasy again when the man shook his head and said, "Goodness, where are my manners? Come on in out of the cold. My name's Reece, Conrad Reece, and I believe the missus might have some coffee or some hot chocolate to warm you up while we work all this out."

He ushered them into a spacious living room and gestured for them to sit down. The officers both sat in chairs, but the girls sank to the floor in a cluster in front of the roaring fire. Then Mr. Reece disappeared, and Lori could hear him talking to his wife. That's "the missus," she thought. When he came back, Mrs. Reece was with him, and she carried a trayful of steaming mugs, which they handed to the officers and the girls. Gratefully, Lori took a drink of the hot chocolate and felt warmth return to her body.

"Now," said Mr. Reece, frowning as he sat down in his easy chair. "I don't really see any need for the police to get involved in a little

TP-ing incident." Then he glanced toward the girls and chuckled again. "I'm sure you two gentlemen have some real criminals you could be chasing."

Sergeant Logan set his mug on the coffee table. "I'm afraid that there is a little more to this than just the toilet-paper incident, Mr. Reece."

"Excuse me," Hildy interjected. "But do you think we could use your telephone to call my father? If he told you who I am, that would probably take care of everything. Wouldn't it, Sergeant O'Donnell?"

"I think it would. Sir, may we use it?"

"Of course. Come with me."

Mr. Reece rose and led Hildy and Sergeant O'Donnell out of the room. Lori focused on her cup of hot chocolate as if it were the most fascinating thing in the world. She was dying to know how Hildy's father was taking the news that his own daughter had stolen the car.

When they all returned to the room a few minutes later, Hildy's smile was as bright as ever. "Everything's cool," she announced. "Daddy identified me as his own little prodigal and told me to bring the car right home. Thanks again, Mr. Reece. Thanks for being so understanding, too. We'll make sure every last bit of toilet paper is out of your trees."

"Would it be okay if we cleaned them up Sunday afternoon?" asked Lori. "I'm signed up to go on the all-school ski trip to Vail tomorrow."

"Oh, gosh, I am, too," said Candi.

"Sunday would be just fine," he assured her.

"And be sure to let us know you're here," added Mrs. Reece. "I'll warm you up with some more hot chocolate."

Lori felt as though she might collapse as they all climbed back into Hildy's car for the ride home. It had been an incredible evening, and she was exhausted.

"Hildy Franklin. You're an absolute nut!" said Candi. "You can talk your way out of anything. You have more nerve than anybody I ever met."

"You can say that again," agreed Meg. "I thought I'd die when that officer asked to see your driver's license."

"Hildy, how on earth can you get away with driving home?" Lori asked. "You don't have a license. What did you do?"

"Absolutely nothing! I kept changing the subject until I faked them out," she answered confidently. "And faking it is the name of the game."

Chapter 9

"Faking it is the name of the game." Hildy's words echoed in Lori's mind the next morning all through the ride to school in the predawn darkness. She had had a lesson in faking it from a real pro last night, and today was going to be the first big test of what she had learned.

The yellow school bus was already waiting under a light post when Mrs. Byrum swung the family's silver and maroon van into the seniors' parking lot. A dozen students clad in brightly colored ski clothes milled around the bus. They huddled in the cold morning air and stamped their feet on the frozen ground. At least I look the part, Lori thought, zipping her lavender-and-yellow ski jacket up a little higher. The only thing that would give away her amateur status was the rental numbers painted on the bottoms of her skis. She vowed to stay on her feet no matter what it took. She kissed her mother good-bye, shouldered her skis, and headed for the bus.

Lori was looking around for Jody when she heard someone behind her call her name.

"Lori! Over here." It was Candi Dawson, and she was signaling furiously at Lori to join her and the small group that had formed near the front of the bus. "I was just telling all these kids about last night."

Lori cringed. Jody had just stepped out of a sporty little compact and was taking her gear off the ski rack. She was well within hearing range of Candi, and she waved to Lori as she walked toward the bus. Lori didn't want Jody to hear about last night's escapade. She was as straight as anyone could get. Jody probably wouldn't think much of Lori if she knew Lori had almost gotten picked up by the police.

"Come on, Lori," Candi insisted. "They don't believe me. Tell them how we TP-ed the wrong house and how Hildy faked the cops into thinking she had a driver's license after they almost arrested her for stealing her own car."

"Sure, it's all true," Lori said, laughing. "And then we were attacked by pygmy headhunters, but King Kong saved us by carrying us up the side of the Empire State Building."

Everyone joined her in the laughter. Candi just gave Lori a puzzled look. Lori didn't care. If it kept Jody from taking the story seriously, it was definitely worth it. After all, she couldn't deny what had happened in front of Candi.

"What was that all about?" Jody asked as she leaned her skis against the bus. "The police. Pygmy headhunters. King Kong. It sounded like a great evening. I'd like to hear more about it."

"Oh, Candi was just trying to kid everyone," said Lori. "She has a wild sense of humor."

Jody seemed satisfied, and Mrs. Crocker, the girls' gym teacher and faculty adviser for the Girls' Athletic Association, held up her hand for quiet. "I think just about everybody is here. As I call off your name, you can board the bus. Jody Atterberry. Lori Byrum. Rod Springer. Craig Jordan . . ."

Jody scooted into a seat midway back in the bus, and Lori sank down beside her. It didn't take long for the bus to fill up with noisy skiers. The driver loaded the equipment and started the bus. They embarked on the three-and-a-half-hour ride to Vail just as the sun began to light the sky with a peachy glow.

The trip was uneventful. Most kids slept, and Lori dozed a few times. She woke up with a start once after dreaming she was whooshing down the mountain at breakneck speed.

Lori and Jodi had barely stretched their legs and collected their gear when Rod and Craig skied to a stop beside them. The boys had already gotten their lift tickets and were ready to head for the slopes.

"Does that promise still hold to race us down the new expert tracks?" Rod asked with a grin.

"Race!" gasped Lori. "We didn't say anything about racing."

"Sure you did," insisted Craig, but he was grinning, too, and Lori knew that they were only kidding.

"I'll tell you what, guys. You two go on up and practice awhile," said Jody. She looked at

Lori and winked. "Lori and I will give you a fifteen-minute head start, and then we'll meet you at the top. But if you get up there and it looks too tough, just tell us, and we'll understand."

"You've got a deal," said Craig, "about meeting you at the top, that is. Nothing is too tough for us."

Rod gave a war whoop in agreement, and they pushed off. Lori breathed a sigh of relief. A fifteen-minute reprieve wasn't much, but she'd gladly take whatever she could get.

Suddenly Jody stopped and turned toward her. "Gosh, Lori, I wasn't thinking. I want to stop by the pro shop and get my bindings checked, but you're probably anxious to get to the slopes. You should have gone up with the guys. Maybe if you hurry, you can catch them."

"Oh, I'm in no hurry," Lori assured her. "You go ahead. I'll wait for you right here."

Jody hurried off toward the pro shop, and Lori sank down onto a log bench outside the back entrance to the lodge. Skiers in bright jackets dotted the mountainside, and a giant cloud of steam rose over the heated swimming pool behind the lodge. Despite the scenery, all Lori could think about was the ordeal ahead. Her eyes followed the ascending chair lift and picked out a girl in a green jacket riding alone in one of the chairs. Maybe if I watch her get off the lift and ski down the hill, I'll see how easy it really is and not be so scared, she thought. When she reached the top, the girl skied off the lift with ease and began a graceful descent. That doesn't look so hard, Lori thought. Her confidence began to return.

"Oh, Lori. There you are. I've been looking all over for you," said Candi. She didn't seem upset by Lori's earlier story to the other kids. She was carrying her skis in an awkward *X* across the front of her body while her boots dangled precariously from her shoulder. "If you don't have anybody to ski with, maybe you'd like to come over to the bunny slopes with me. I'm a terrible skier. This is only the second time I've tried it, and I need someone to give me moral support. Besides," she added reluctantly, "the ski patrol just brought some turkey down on a stretcher. They think he probably has a broken leg. I'd die if I broke my leg. I wouldn't be able to cheerlead the rest of the year."

Lori felt a rising tide of panic. The mountain had only been open for skiing less than thirty minutes and already someone had a broken leg. What on earth was she doing here? Making friends with someone was one thing, she thought, but not if it meant killing yourself in the process. Then she felt a spark of hope. Here was her way out. Poor Candi needed help. And wouldn't Jody be impressed that she would give up a fabulous day on the slopes to help a beginner conquer her fears? Lori tried to think of every angle. How much more complicated could this business get? What if it backfired and she blew her big chance to impress Jody?

"Gee, Candi. I was supposed to ski with Jody Atterberry . . ."

"That jock!" cried Candi. "Oh, come on, Lori.

Do you want to get killed? Let's face it, you may be able to ski, but Jody Atterberry is in a class of her own."

"Yeah, that's what I was thinking, too," Lori murmured. Then in a louder voice she said, "Of course it probably wouldn't hurt me to warm up a little bit on the bunny slope. I haven't been on skis for an awfully long time. Wait here while I tell Jody to go on up to the top without me this time."

Jody was coming out the door when Lori reached the pro shop. "Listen, Jody," Lori began. "Candi Dawson asked me to ski with her on the bunny slope for a little while, and I think I should. She's a real beginner, and she just saw the ski patrol bring down a guy with a broken leg. It really shook her up, so I told her I would ski with her until she felt better. You don't mind, do you?"

"Gee, no. Maybe I should come along, too," Jody offered.

"No, that's okay. I can handle it. Besides, Rod and Craig are waiting at the top. Tell them I'll be up as soon as I can leave Candi. Okay?"

Jody's expression softened into one of understanding. "Sure. And Lori. That's really great of you. I know Candi will certainly appreciate it. Catch you later."

Lori watched Jody head for the chair lifts feeling as if she had just been granted a stay of execution. She wouldn't have to make a fool of herself after all, and Jody thought she was some kind of hero.

Candi was waiting for Lori at the bottom of

the bunny slope. She had put on her skis and was ready to go up. Lori slipped her boots into her bindings and glanced toward the tow rope that carried skiers to the top of the beginner area. She tried to look casual, but she was studying the lift and how the skiers used it.

It looked simple enough. Each skier would step into well-worn tracks beside a small building that housed the motor and other gear. Then the skier would grab hold of the rope and be pulled up to the top. Every now and then someone would let go of the rope too early and sit down in the snow. When that happened the man operating the tow would stop the machinery until the skier had moved clear of the tracks. Then he would turn the motor on again, and the rest of the riders would continue up the slope.

"Ready to go up?" asked Candi.

"You bet," Lori answered confidently. "Let's go."

Lori purposely ignored the sign tacked to the building which said: "If you have never ridden this lift before, ask your operator for assistance." The operator was a bear of a man with a thick red beard. She would die before she would ask him for help, especially in front of Candi.

They joined the short line waiting to ride the tow, and when it came her turn, Candi stepped up and grabbed on to the rope. "This is the easy part," she called over her shoulder as she began moving up the hill.

Lori took a deep breath and started to step into the tracks behind Candi, but the operator held up his hand for her to stop. "Remove your poles and hold them in one hand," he instructed. "It's dangerous to keep the straps around your wrists when you ride the tow."

Lori stepped back and let the line move around her while she followed his orders. By the time Lori stepped back into the tracks, Candi was at the top of the hill. "Gently squeeze the rope and let it pull you," the operator said in a monotonous tone, and Lori wondered briefly how many times a day he must say that same thing.

She put her hands around the rope and took hold, jerking forward. This isn't too bad, she told herself. The track was icy, and her skis clattered as they bumped along it, but otherwise she was ascending smoothly toward the top of the hill.

Suddenly her left ski hit a loose chunk of ice and left the track. Lori tightened her grip on the rope and tried to pull her ski back where it belonged. She had to let go as she lost her balance completely and pitched forward onto the icy track.

"Oh, no!" she cried as she spun around on the slippery surface. Then, to her horror, she began to slide backward, picking up speed as she shot headfirst down the hill. Skiers who had been behind her on the tow plunged into the snow, ducking away from her flailing skis. Her bindings released the skis from her boots, but the safety straps prevented the skis from sliding away. The tow-rope house was getting closer, and the operator's hands reached for her. Then she came to a sudden stop in darkness.

She lay there in a daze for a moment, listening to the sound of excited voices but unable to understand where she was.

"Get the ski patrol!"

"Is she hurt?"

"She's under the tow-rope house!"

"How did she get under there?"

Lori raised her head and looked into the slit of light that appeared between her outstretched legs. She gasped. Oh, my gosh. I really am under the tow-rope house, she thought. Only her feet, with skis dangling nearby, extended past the darkness of the tiny cavern where she lay.

Suddenly a red beard blotted out most of the light. "Are you okay, miss? Can you move?"

"Get me out of here!" Lori cried in sudden panic. She tried to scoot toward the light, but the space was too tiny to maneuver in.

"Hang in there. We're getting the ski patrol. They'll get you out."

"Get me out of here!"

"The ski patrol will be here any minute. We'd better not move you until they make sure you aren't hurt."

Lori lay back and closed her eyes. She knew she wasn't hurt, not physically anyway. But how would she ever face anybody again? At least Jody hadn't witnessed her humiliation. But Candi had, and she would tell everybody.

Finally the ski patrol arrived. "How do you feel, miss? Do you hurt anywhere?"

Lori could see the face of the young man who

was speaking. He looked about college age and was terribly good-looking in his rust-colored ski-patrol jacket.

"I'm perfectly fine. Just get me out of here. *Please,*" she begged.

She held her breath as strong hands grabbed hold of each foot and slowly pulled her into the open air. Lori was asked again if she were hurt. Shaking her head, she saw for the first time that a large crowd of skiers had gathered to watch. They were silent until she was finally able to sit up, and then they began to cheer wildly.

She could hear the lift operator explaining what had happened to a curious skier. He remarked that he had never seen anybody slide under the lift house before, and then he laughed loudly. Lori didn't look up. Instead she worked on unbuckling the safety straps. She wished desperately that they would all go away and leave her alone.

Finally the crowd dispersed and she noticed for the first time that Candi wasn't anywhere around. Lori got to her feet quickly and scanned the slope for signs of her friend. Suddenly Candi came into view, skiing very slowly down the slope with her tips pointed together. When she came to a stop beside Lori, she was smiling broadly.

"I must have missed you at the top," she said, brushing snow from her jacket. "I fell down just behind those trees up there, and it took me all this time to get up again. Boy, was that hard work!"

Lori couldn't believe her good fortune. Candi

didn't even know. Nobody knew because Lori and Candi had been the only kids from the bus to head for the beginner slope. She had put one over on everyone, after all!

Chapter 10

Lori pretended her ankle was twisted and sat in the lodge the rest of the day sipping Cokes and watching the other skiers. The twisted ankle had been an easy thing to fake since Candi had assumed that Lori made at least one run down the slope while she was struggling to get up after her fall.

"Took a header and really messed up my ankle," Lori had said without the slightest twinge of guilt. There was no way on earth that she was going to get back on that tow rope.

Her only bad moment came in the bus on the way home when Rod Springer announced that he had heard that some amateur with numbers on the bottoms of her skis had slid under the tow-rope house on the bunny slope. The entire bus broke up with laughter.

She and Jody sat together again on the way home, and Jody filled her in on the day's skiing.

"You really should have been there, Lori. Those new expert slopes are murder! And you

88

should have seen the expressions on Rod and
Craig's faces when they started down them for
the first time. They both looked scared to death."

Lori breathed a secret sigh of relief. "I'm
sorry I missed that," she lied.

When the bus pulled into the parking lot,
Lori retrieved her skis, carrying them so that no
one could see the numbers on the bottoms. She
headed for the pay telephone across the street
to call home for a ride.

"Wait up," called Jody. She sprinted over to
join Lori and nodded toward the phone where
a line was beginning to form. "I have to call,
too."

They walked along in silence. Then Jody
brightened and said, "I'm glad to see that your
ankle is so much better. You aren't limping
anymore."

Lori winced. She had forgotten all about her
ankle. "It feels a lot better. In fact, it hardly
hurts at all."

"That's good," said Jody. "But jogging probably wouldn't be good for it yet."

Puzzled, Lori said, "Jogging?"

Jody nodded. "A group of us jog on the Fairview track every Sunday around noon. When
we're finished we go have lunch. I was going to
ask if you'd like to go along tomorrow, but with
your ankle . . ."

"Oh, it really is a lot better," Lori interrupted.
She wouldn't miss a chance like that for anything. "Actually, I was feeling so much better by
the middle of the afternoon that I considered
coming up to the expert slopes and skiing with

you guys for a while, but I decided not to push it. I'm sure that by tomorrow it will be in perfect shape for jogging."

"Great," said Jody. "Meet me at the track at noon. We'll do five miles or so and then get some lunch. It will be fun to have you along. Jessica Mills will probably be there and some of the other girls from the basketball team. We try to get a group together because running alone can be pretty boring."

Lori smiled weakly. Five miles? She wanted to ask Jody if she meant five miles without stopping, but she was sure she already knew the answer.

She was almost ready to leave for the track the next morning when the phone rang.

"Lori! It's for you," her mother called up from downstairs.

Picking up the upstairs extension, she said. "Hello,"

"Hi, Lori. It's Hildy. Don't forget that we have to pull all the toilet paper out of Mr. Reece's trees this afternoon."

Oh, no, thought Lori. She had forgotten.

"Lori? Are you there?"

"Sure, Hildy. I'm here. And I did forget about Mr. Reece's trees," she confessed. "What time were you going to do it?"

"How about two o'clock? Trish will be busy until then because it's her little sister's birthday, and her grandparents are coming to dinner right after church," Hildy said.

"Two o'clock?" Could she possibly be finished

jogging and eating lunch by then? She had no idea how long it took to run five miles. "Can I meet you over there? I might be just a little late."

"Sure." Hildy sounded laid back. "We're riding our bikes over. Then if it isn't dark yet when we're finished, we're going to Pisano's Pizza, so bring some money."

"Terrific!" said Lori. "I'll see you at Reeces'. Bye."

Lori couldn't believe her good fortune. Lunch with Jody and pizza with Hildy, both in the same day. The temperature was well below the freezing mark, so Lori dressed as warmly as possible. She put on two pairs of socks, her ski underwear, cords, two sweaters, her ski jacket, knit hat, and mittens. There, she thought, surveying herself in the mirror. I look a little roly-poly, but I ought to stay warm.

Jody was already at the track doing deep knee bends when Lori arrived on her bike a little while later. None of the other girls was there yet. "Warming up," Jody called, smiling broadly.

Lori locked her bike to a tree and joined Jody. "Guess I'd better warm up a little myself," she said. She raised her arms and bent forward to touch her toes, but her bulky clothing stopped her halfway down. Puffing, she pushed harder and reached her fingertips downward, but it was no use. Jody was watching her, and Lori smiled sheepishly as she stood upright again.

Jody shook her head. "Why on earth are you wearing so many clothes? You're going to roast once we start running. Look at me. All I have on are sweats and a windbreaker plus my hat and gloves, and I'm comfortable."

"You're probably right. I don't usually run in such cold weather. Besides, I think I warmed up my muscles pretty well riding over here on my bike."

Jody seemed satisfied. "Okay," she said. "We don't have to wait for the others. If you're ready, let's get started. This is a quarter-mile track, so we'll go around it twenty times."

Twenty times! Lori almost gasped out loud. The thought was staggering. She would be lucky if she made it around twice. It was obvious that Ms. Jock was ready to go. She was running in place while she waited for Lori to join her. Lori took a deep breath and trotted out onto the track. She was determined to go through with this. She would pace herself, running as slowly as possible, and do all twenty laps if it killed her.

They started around at a slow pace. This isn't too bad, thought Lori. She was concentrating hard on trying to stay loose, and it took her a minute to realize that Jody was talking to her.

"I'm really glad to find someone else who likes skiing and running as much as I do," she was saying. "Unfortunately there aren't too many girls who are into those things the way we are. I have to admit, though, that you really surprised me. I always thought you were so quiet."

Lori gave a nervous little laugh. "Not really," she said. "It's just that I used to go around with Monica Carrol most of the time, and she doesn't care for any of this."

Jody's expression was concerned. Lori added quickly, "Monica and I are still friends, but I decided it was time to do my own thing."

"Good for you," said Jody turning thumbs up in a victory sign, and Lori felt good. She was making points. An instant later her spirits sank again as Jody called out, "Lap one. Only nineteen to go."

Lori tried to put one foot in front of the other and not think about the five miles. But her heart was pounding from exertion, and her chest was beginning to ache. She could feel perspiration rolling down her back, and the calves of her legs were tightening. How could she ever last for nineteen more laps.?

To her left, the shadow of another runner appeared on the macadam. It was moving forward, gaining on her.

"Hi, Lori. How's it going?" Jessica Mills called out as she sprinted past Lori. She was a tall girl, more athletic-looking than Jody, and she was in front and out of hearing range before Lori could attempt to answer her.

"Lap two," shouted Jody. She was smiling broadly at Lori, obviously loving every minute.

Managing a weak smile in response, Lori tried to remember everything she had ever read about jogging. Wasn't there something about getting your second wind? she wondered. Surely she was overdue for hers. Suddenly pictures of exhausted marathon runners crowded into her mind. She had seen them on television at least a dozen times. There were runners collapsing into the arms of spectators. Runners lying on the grass, panting as if they were dying for breath. Runners staggering over the finish line on wobbling legs. Now she knew how every one of them felt.

"Lap three!" Jody sang out. An instant later she waved toward the street and called, "Hey there, Tripp."

Lori could see Tripp Lefcoe out of the corner of her eye. He was standing beside the track watching the girls run by. She raised her arm to wave to him just as a searing pain tore through her side. She stopped, doubling over, as it subsided for an instant and then returned to throb angrily.

Jody and Tripp were at her side in a second. Breathless, she put an arm over each of their shoulders and used them like crutches to hobble to the edge of the track.

"It's a good thing I stopped by," said Tripp as he helped her down onto the grass. "I was on my way home from the library when I saw you jogging."

"It's your ankle, isn't it?" Jody demanded. "I was afraid this might happen." Then turning to Tripp, she added, "Lori hurt her ankle skiing yesterday, but she insisted on jogging with me today anyway."

"Which ankle is it?" asked Tripp. There was genuine worry in his voice. Lori felt a twinge of guilt. "We should check it for swelling."

For an instant Lori couldn't remember which foot she had limped on the day before. Jody would remember, so she had to get it right.

"My left one," she said.

Tripp knelt and raised her left foot, pressing the ankle gently and then rotating her foot. "It seems okay, but I'd be careful it I were you. You probably ought to stay off it for at least the rest of the day."

Jody nodded. "I agree."

Jessica Mills loped over to the sidelines. "What's the matter? Somebody hurt?"

"It's Lori, Jes," said Jody. "She hurt her ankle, but she'll be okay." Then turning back to Lori, she added, "I should never have let you come jogging on it in the first place. I'm awfully sorry Lori. It's all my fault."

Jody looked so miserable that for a moment Lori was tempted to confess. But she couldn't do that. It would spoil everything. Jody really cares about people, thought Lori. No wonder she wanted Jody for a friend.

"It's not your fault, silly," said Lori. "I just turned it or something. I agree that I shouldn't jog anymore today, but it's going to be fine."

"Then I won't jog anymore either. Jes and the others can go on without us, and we'll get some lunch. Tripp, why don't you come with us. We're going to Yogurt Heaven."

Tripp made a face. "Yogurt Heaven?" he muttered. Then he turned to Lori and said, "Do you eat that stuff?"

"Oh, sure. All the time. I'm really into health food," she lied.

Tripp made another face. "If you'd said a burger and fries, it would have been one thing. But yogurt! Count me out. I'll see you around."

Lori watched Tripp gather up his library

books, wave back toward them, and head for home. She wished that he were coming with them. She always felt so comfortable when he was around. A burger and fries sounded great to her, too, but she was stuck with Yogurt Heaven. Yuk! she thought. Skiing, jogging, and yogurt. This friendship is costing me a lot.

Chapter 11

Yogurt Heaven was almost deserted. Lori had never been inside before and was surprised at the cozy ice-cream-parlor decor. She ordered a strawberry parfait at the counter and joined Jody at a round table for two with wire-back chairs and red-and-white-striped seats. She could practically taste a big, delicious burger and warm, salty fries, and she felt certain that the small cup of pink yogurt that the waitress brought her would do little to quiet her growling stomach.

"You know, Lori," Jody said, punctuating the air with her plastic spoon. "As I said while we were running, I'm really glad to find out that you like the same kinds of things that I do. It just amazes me that so many kids waste their lives lying around listening to rock music and consuming mountains of junk food when there are so many really great things they could be doing. Do you know what I mean?"

"Sure," said Lori. She popped a spoonful of

yogurt into her mouth and wanted to change the subject.

"I don't mean to knock music," Jody went on. "Sometimes I listen to it, too, but they don't hand out college scholarships based upon the number of albums you own. If I can get a basketball scholarship to a good school, then I can major in premed and hopefully become a doctor. I can never make it without that scholarship, though. My parents don't have that kind of money. Plus," she added with a laugh, "they have three more kids besides me to educate."

"Well, if anyone can do it, you can," Lori said with genuine admiration. She was certain that the word *fail* wasn't even in Jody Atterberry's vocabulary.

Jody shrugged. "So what are your plans for after high school?" she asked.

Lori felt cornered. "I haven't really decided yet," she confessed. It was true. In fact, she didn't have any idea what she wanted to do with her life. She had thought that she still had plenty of time to worry about that, but Jody had plans already. Maybe she should say something like nuclear physics or something. She almost choked on a giggle at the thought.

"What's so funny?" asked Jody.

"Nothing much. I was just imagining myself as a nuclear physicist."

"Don't laugh. You could be one if you really wanted to. There's nothing we can't do if we want it."

Lori scraped the last of the pink yogurt from the bottom of her cup and remembered that she was suppposed to meet Hildy and the others at the Reeces' house at two o'clock. She glanced at her watch. It was five minutes past two.

"Eek!" she said. "I didn't realize it had gotten so late. I was supposed to be somewhere five minutes ago."

"Can you make it okay?" asked Jody. "I mean is your ankle strong enough?"

"Sure. It's a lot better. Besides I have my bike outside." Lori paused and then added, "I really had fun today. I'm glad you asked me to come along."

Jody looked pleased. "We'll do it again next Sunday if your ankle is well by then. And, Lori . . . I didn't mean to preach a sermon. I just get carried away sometimes. I promise not to bug you to be a nuclear physicist either."

Both girls were laughing as they said goodbye. Lori remembered to limp just slightly as she left Yogurt Heaven and got on her bike. She thought about her conversation with Jody as she pedaled toward the Reeces' house. Jody was probably right. She could do anything she put her mind to—anything except jogging five miles! There was something else on her mind, too. Making friends with Jody just wasn't as much fun as she had thought it would be. Not that there is anything wrong with exercise and health food, she thought. But they weren't at the top of her list of favorite things.

She burst out laughing as she rounded the corner into Buckingham Court and caught sight of the Reeces' front yard. The pink streamers hanging from the trees would have been funny enough, but what made her really laugh was the sight of Hildy, Trish, Candi, and Meg, all wandering around the yard angling long bamboo fishing poles into the trees as they tried to snag the toilet paper. Their necks were craned so that they could see the upper branches of the trees, and just as Lori stopped her bike beside the others lined up in the driveway, Hildy and Meg smacked into each other. They lost their balance, and both girls sprawled to the ground.

"Do you guys realize how crazy you look?" asked Lori. "I'd give anything for a camera. I could blackmail all of you for life."

Everyone was laughing, but Hildy looked up at Lori and said in mock seriousness, "Don't laugh until *you* try it."

"In fact, you get your chance right now," said Candi. "Mr. Reece put a fishing pole for you over by the garage door."

Lori wondered if the Reeces or any of their neighbors were looking out of their windows as she picked up her pole and joined the others. They would certainly be getting a good laugh if they were. She went to work on one of the trees nearest the house and soon understood what Hildy had meant about not laughing until she tried it. The length of the pole made it awkward to handle, and it bent in the breeze.

"I see what you mean about Charmin sticking to the branches," she muttered as she poked away at a streamer that clung stubbornly to a branch over her head.

The girls worked in silence for a while until

the lawn looked as though it had been hit by a pink snowstorm. Finally, they brought down all but a few tatters that hung to the topmost limbs and tied the rest securely into plastic leaf bags. They called Mr. Reece out for his inspection.

"Well done," he said. His expression was serious at first, but soon his eyes began to twinkle and he chuckled to himself before he spoke again, "But the next time you want to shower me with affection, why not just send a greeting card instead?" With that he began laughing so hard that the girls had to join in.

"Won't you come inside for some hot chocolate?" asked Mrs. Reece, who had come out with her husband. "It's no trouble."

"Thanks," said Hildy. "But it's getting late. I think we'd better get going."

To Pisano's, I hope, thought Lori. The strawberry yogurt parfait she had had for lunch had not made a dent in her hunger, and her stomach was rumbling like thunder.

The sidewalk in front of Pisano's was littered with bicycles when they arrived a few minutes later. Inside it was so crowded that they couldn't find a table.

They stayed near the door to wait for a table to empty, until Hildy announced an idea. "You guys stay here and keep your eyes peeled for someone leaving, and I'll go scout. Surely there's somebody we can sit with."

She disappeared into the crowd just as someone played a Police song on the jukebox. Lori hummed along, inhaling the great aroma of Papa Manetti's pizza. Despite the problems, this had been one of the greatest days of her life. A moment later Hildy was back. She was rocking to the music and grinning.

"Did I tell you that there was someone here that we can sit with? Did I? Huh?" she asked with a rippling laugh. "Well, you know that little ole Hildy always tells the truth."

"So, don't keep us in suspense," said Trish. "Who is it?"

Hildy raked her fingers through her short red hair as if she had nothing else to do, and Lori knew that keeping them in suspense was exactly what she was doing. It must be someone pretty special, Lori thought.

"Ed Beachley." Hildy spoke the name at the exact instant that Lori guessed it, and her heart began to pound as Hildy went on. "Ed is here and so are Rod Springer and Craig Jordan, and they have a huge booth way at the back. There's plenty of room for all of us. Come on. Follow me."

Lori was too paralyzed to move. Ed Beachley was here, and she would be sitting in the same booth with him. Her hand flew to her face. She must look terrible. She had purposely not worn makeup to jog with Jody, and she had forgotten to stop along the way to the Reeces' and put some on. Her hair must look awful, too, and her clothes! She had put on so many extra layers to keep warm that she looked like a blimp. She couldn't let Ed see her this way.

"Come on, Lori. Move." Trish was behind her, and as the others followed Hildy into the crowd, she nudged Lori to follow, too.

"I'm going to duck into the ladies' room. I'll be there in a minute."

Lori began peeling off layers of clothing as soon as the ladies' room door closed behind her. She stuffed them out of sight behind the overflowing trash can. She would worry about them later. Then she dug around in her purse until she found her hairbrush, mascara, and lip gloss. Her hands were shaking from the anticipation of being with Ed Beachley. Finally she was able to stand back and look approvingly at her reflection in the mirror. "I'm ready," she whispered, and walked back into the crowded restaurant.

"Hi, Lori. Looking for someplace to sit?"

It was Angela Manetti, and she was wearing an apron smudged with tomato sauce carrying one large pizza in each hand.

"Oh, hi, Angela. No thanks. I'm with a big group of kids, and we're sitting in a booth at the back."

Lori moved through the crowd, thinking how great it was to be seen with Hildy and her friends. She had been tempted to tell Angela who she was with just to see the look on her face. But Angela would probably wait on them, and then she would find out.

She had only to follow the sound of Hildy's laughter to find the large, circular booth where her friends were sitting. Hildy was sitting next to Ed at the very back. The girls were crammed in next to her on one side and the guys lounged on the other. Everybody scooted around when she got there, creating a small space next to

Meg. Lori wedged herself into the space, thinking that Ed looked handsome. His sandy blond hair was cut short on top, but in back it was longer, coming together in a rat tail and curled onto the back of his Van Halen sweat shirt.

"Hey, Lori. How's your ankle?"

Craig Jordan's words brought her back to reality. "Super," she said. "Jody told me that I really missed a wild time up on those new expert slopes."

"Is that girl a jock twenty-four hours a day, or what?" asked Hildy. She had a disgusted look on her face. "I mean she is dull, dull, *dull*. She's either studying or playing some dumb sport all the time."

"That's what she likes to do," said Lori. "And she has some pretty high goals for herself."

"Yeah. But she's missing all the fun. And what for?" asked Hildy. "I say you have to enjoy life while you can, and speaking of enjoying life, I just gave Ed the word on your connections with Duran Duran."

Lori shot her a horrified look.

"I know, I wasn't supposed to tell anybody," said Hildy. She looked beseechingly at Lori. "But I just had to tell Ed about it since he was *supposed* to be taking me to the concert."

"Tell us more about this cool cousin of yours. What's his name? How do we get to meet him?" asked Rod.

"C'mon, c'mon," coaxed Craig.

Lori felt her face flush as all eyes around the table were on her. This whole thing was getting out of hand. It had been hard enough to invent an imaginary cousin for Hildy when Lori knew she didn't have a prayer of producing him, or the tickets. Now Hildy was broadcasting it to the whole school. What on earth am I going to do? she thought. Hang in there, she told herself. There was nothing she could do but go along with it for now.

"His name is Chris Byrum, and he's my third cousin on my mother's side. I've only seen him once or twice in my life."

"How could he be your third cousin on your mother's side if his last name is Byrum?" asked Meg.

"Oh, I meant on my father's side," sputtered Lori. She was getting more and more flustered by the minute.

"Any chance you can get us some tickets for the concert?" asked Rod.

"*If* he really exists," said Craig pointedly.

"Lor, show them the letter," insisted Hildy. "They'll believe you when they see that."

"Gee. It's at home. Oh, here comes Angela," she said, trying to keep the relief out of her voice. "Is everybody ready to order?"

Angela took their orders, and Lori could tell by the expression on her face that she was pretty impressed to see Lori with such a popular crowd. The conversation drifted to other things as they ate pizza and listened to music on the jukebox. Lori was beginning to relax. She was going to get away with her little charade one more time.

Lori took a bite of her pepperoni pizza and strung the cheese out in front of her. Suddenly she was looking straight into Ed Beachley's eyes.

He was staring at her intently, almost daring her to look away. A tiny thrill hit her. Why was he staring at her like that? Ed had the most gorgeous blue eyes of any guy she knew. Like limpid pools, they always said in poetry. She wondered briefly what *limpid* meant. It didn't really matter, she decided. Whatever it meant, that was definitely what his eyes were like.

"Hey, it's getting late," said Candi. "If we're going to ride our bikes home before dark, we'd better get going."

Lori glanced toward the window. Candi was right. The late afternoon sunshine was fading. The crowd in Pisano's had thinned out, she noticed, as they lined up in front of the cashier. Most of the tables were empty now, still littered with pizza crusts, soda glasses, and crumpled napkins. For the second time, Lori felt as if someone was staring at her. She glanced back at Ed, but he and Hildy were deep in conversation. Lori looked around uncomfortably until she spotted the person whose eyes were on her. She relaxed. It was Tripp. He was on the other side of the room. Then Lori noticed that the other person at the table with him was Jillian Glenn, a popular freshman who was on Candi Dawson's junior varsity cheerleading squad.

Tripp looked away from Lori and began talking to Jillian. Lori felt a sudden stab of anger. Or was it hurt? She tried to brush it away as silly. After all, she reasoned, she and Tripp were just good friends.

Lori shot another quick look at Jillian and Tripp. Was Jillian the real reason he had turned down the offer to go to Yogurt Heaven with her and Jody earlier?

She was still thinking about Tripp and Jillian when she left Pisano's, but as she started to get on her bike, Ed Beachley stepped in front of it, straddling the front wheel and gripping the handlebars. Hildy and the others had already gone, and Lori felt a blush spread across her face as she looked at him.

"So you've got a cousin who's a roadie for Duran Duran," he said. Then he smiled such a fantastic smile that her heart went wheeling off into space.

All she could do was nod.

"That's great. You'll have to tell me more about him one of these times."

He released her bike then, and she headed home feeling as though she were flying a plane instead of pedaling a bike. Ed Beachley had noticed her, and he had almost made a pass at her. It was fantastic. A week ago her world had seemed dismal. Today things were looking up. She felt so happy she could easily ignore that her friendships were all based on pretending.

Chapter 12

Music greeted Lori as she entered the house a few minutes later. It was the kind of music Lori heard on elevators. She made a face and wondered for the millionth time how her parents could listen to that drippy stuff. Since it was Sunday night and the elevator music was on, they were probably in the living room playing Scrabble and eating popcorn. That had been their Sunday night routine ever since she could remember.

Lori tiptoed past the living-room door, headed for the privacy of her room. She wasn't in the mood for how-was-your-day type conversation. She wanted to think about Ed Beachley and her afternoon with Jody and Hildy.

But more important than that, on the way home from Pisano's a plan for getting tickets to the Duran Duran concert had begun to take shape in her mind. Her father did a lot of business with people in Denver. Once he had gotten tickets through one of his clients to see some opera star after the concert was sold out. Maybe he knew someone who could get tickets for Duran Duran. If he could, she would really be in tight with Hildy and Ed Beachley and their crowd. Of course, it was only a possibility. In fact, it might not work at all, but she wanted time to think it through before she said anything to her father.

"Lori? Is that you?" her mother called. Lori backed up into the living room. She faced her parents, who were sitting on the floor before a roaring fire. The Scrabble board was between them, and a large bowl of popcorn sat to one side.

"Yeah, Mom. Just coming in."

Mrs. Byrum smiled warmly. "How was your day?"

"Great!"

"That's good, dear. Are you hungry? There's some cold roast beef in the fridge."

"No, thanks. I went to Pisano's with Hildy Franklin and some of her friends."

"Speaking of friends," Mr. Byrum interjected, "Monica called. In fact, she called a couple of times. She wants you to call her back."

"Thanks, Dad. I'll do it right now."

She started to leave the room and stopped. Maybe she should go ahead and talk to her father about the concert tickets right now while he was relaxed.

"Dad," she said. "Remember a couple of years ago when you got tickets for that opera star's concert from one of your friends in Denver?"

"You mean Luciano Pavarotti. Yes, I remember. The gentleman who got the tickets is a client of mine, and he's also a big opera fan."

Lori's heart sank. No way was her father's client going to be able to get tickets to a concert by a hot group like Duran Duran. "Oh, well," she said. "So much for that idea. I guess you can't help after all."

Mr. Byrum smiled sympathetically. "Tell me what you need. You know I'll help if I can."

"Well," she began. "Duran Duran is one of the biggest rock groups in the world right now. They're from England and they're giving a concert at McNichols Sports Arena in Denver next month, but it was an instant sellout. Some of my friends and I are dying to go, and I thought just maybe . . ." she trailed off.

Mr. Byrum was thoughtful for a moment. "Durant Durant, you say, at McNichols? I can't say for sure, but I could make a few calls."

Lori ran to her father and gave him a big hug. "Thanks a million, Dad. And it's Duran Duran. There's no *T* on the end."

"No promises," he called after her as she hurried out of the room. "And don't forget to call Monica."

"Gotcha!" Lori frowned as she dialed Monica's number. Calling Monica was the last thing in the world she wanted to do. Monica had picked the worst time to call. What could she want from Lori, anyway? She had her big romance with Steve Jones. She's probably bursting with love and just has to tell someone again.

Monica answered after the first ring. "Hello," she said.

"Hi Monica. It's Lori. Dad said you called."

"Oh, Lori. I'm so glad you called me back. Hold on a minute while I move this phone into the closet. I don't want my parents to overhear."

There were muffled sounds, and a moment later she was back on the line. "Steve broke up with me last night, Lori."

"You're kidding? What happened? I thought you two were madly in love." But in the back of her mind, Lori remembered seeing Monica and Steve arguing in the hallway at school a few days earlier. Maybe they weren't so madly in love, after all, she thought.

"Oh, Lori. He's been absolutely awful lately. To start with, he's been telling me that I'm possessive, that he never gets to be with the guys anymore. But, gosh, Lori. When two people care about each other, aren't they supposed to want to be together?"

Lori didn't answer for a moment. She had never considered Monica possessive before, but now that Monica had mentioned it herself, the description fit perfectly. It had always been Monica who had kept their friendship exclusive. She had been the one who had steered them away from any real involvement with other kids.

Why didn't I see that before and realize how wrong it was? Lori wondered. To Monica she simply said, "Sure. You're probably right."

"He's been really rotten," Monica went on. "Every time Shana Beaumont comes around, he acts as if I'm not even there. Last night I decided that I'd had it. We were in Pisano's, and Shana came in, and Steve started going after her right there in front of me. It made me furious, and I told him how I felt. I said that if he thought Shana Beaumont was so wonderful, why didn't he start going with her? And do you know what he said then?"

"No. What?"

"He said, 'That sounds like a great idea,' and then he asked for his class ring back!"

"Wow, Monica. I'm really sorry. I know how crazy you are about him. He and Shana won't last. You know what a loudmouth she is. I'll bet he'll come crawling back to you in less than a week."

"Well, I won't take him back!"

"What! What are you talking about, anyway?"

"Lori, I've had it with boys. I don't want to go out with Steve or anybody else ever again. We don't need them. We don't need anybody. You and I had plenty of fun before Steve Jones came along."

Lori stared at the phone.

"Lori, are you there?" Monica asked.

"Yes. Monica, I'll see you in the morning. I'm sorry about Steve," Lori said again. "Good-bye."

"I'm not sorry, *best friend,*" Monica said pointedly. "I'll see you at your locker, okay?"

"Right."

"Okay, Lori. Good-bye." Lori heard the click of the disconnection. It's time for a talk with Purr-vert she thought.

Chapter 13

"Purr-vert, you won't believe what's going on in my life," Lori said as she plopped down on her water bed next to her sleeping cat a few moments later. He perked up his ears at the sound of her voice, slowly opening his amber eyes and revving up his purr until it reached the high decibel range. "You just won't believe it. After all I've done to get Jody and Hildy to like me, Monica wants everything to go back to the way it was before she started going steady with Steve."

Purr-vert yawned and closed his eyes again.

"Well, it may not sound important to you, but I've nearly killed myself impressing those two," Lori scolded, and then she stroked Purr-vert's soft, black fur. She and Monica had been best friends for most of their lives. As hurt as she had been when Monica dumped her to go steady with Steve, their friendship had been too special to simply end forever. "So why am I depressed?"

I know why, she thought. Monica and I have

never kept secrets from each other. We've told each other absolutely everything. "But I could never tell her about all the maneuvering I've been doing, Purr-vert. If she ever found out about how I studied up on pro basketball and the NBA and went skiing and jogging to impress Jody, I'd be so embarrassed that I'd die. And what about the Duran Duran stuff? The letter and my imaginary cousin? She would think that I've lost my mind. I guess I'll just have to try to fool her, too."

Still, Lori didn't move. Deep down she knew that she was kidding herself. That wasn't all that troubled her about resuming her friendship with Monica. Steve had been right when he told Monica that she was too possessive. She had controlled Lori's life for all these years, and Lori had never realized how much she had been missing. Then, when Monica began going steady with Steve, she had tried to control his life, too.

"Purr-vert, I still like Monica a lot, but I don't want to go back to a one-person friendship. I may be goofing up trying to pretend with Jody and Hildy, but I'm having fun!"

Then she added in a quieter tone, "Besides, they're both friends worth having."

Lori heard the phone ring but decided not to run for it. She never got to it first anymore, not since Number Three had decided to make answering the phone into a big contest. A moment later there was a pounding on her bedroom door.

"It's for you *again*," called her little brother. "And don't stay on too long. I'm expecting a call."

Lori purposely took her time getting up and leaving her room just to bug Stan, who stood in the hallway glowering at her.

"Hurry up," he grumbled.

"I'm getting there," she answered. "Who is it, anyway?"

"I don't know. Some nut who called me Number Three and said I'm her lucky charm." He made a face and scowled all the way toward his room.

Lori burst out laughing. "Hildy?" she said as she grabbed the upstairs extension.

"Right! Hey, Lori. Have I ever got some news for you. You really made a big impression on Ed Beachley this afternoon. He was giving me the third degree before we left Pisano's. He was asking all kinds of questions about you, and it wouldn't surprise me if he called you sometime soon and asked you out."

Lori's heart almost stopped. It was too wonderful to be true. Ed Beachley, the gorgeous guy she had had a crush on since she was a freshman, might actually like her, too.

"But isn't he your boyfriend, Hildy?"

"Of course not," said Hildy. "We go out sometimes, but I go out with lots of guys. You won't catch me going steady. There are too many hunks out there to get tied down to just one."

"Then you wouldn't get mad if he asked me out and I said yes?"

"Never!" Hildy replied emphatically. "In fact, maybe we could double."

Lori didn't say anything for a minute. She was remembering all the times she and Monica had talked about double dating with Ed Beachley and Steve Jones. She was thinking how ironic it was that now that she and Ed might actually be going out, Monica and Steve had broken up. *Me and Ed.*

"That would be fun," she said as the excitement returned. "Did he really say that he was going to call me? And what kind of questions did he ask about me?"

"I'll never tell," Hildy teased.

"Come on, Hildy. You have to tell me. I'll die if you don't."

"Okay. If you really want to know. He asked if you have a boyfriend, and if I thought you liked having a good time . . . among other things. And then he asked if I knew why he'd never noticed how cute you were before."

"You're kidding! Ed Beachley said all that?" Lori cradled the phone on her shoulder and hugged herself with joy. It was just too wonderful to be true.

"Listen, Lori. That's not the only reason I called. I was thinking. You are pretty cute and everything, like Ed said, but you really ought to change your look. You know, update it a little. Why don't you get your hair cut short like mine? You'd look fantastic, and I know Ed would like it. You should have heard how he raved when I got mine cut this way."

Lori nearly dropped the phone. She couldn't believe what she was hearing. She couldn't get a punk haircut. Not in a million years.

"Gee, Hildy. I don't know. I'll have to think about it."

"What's to think about? Like I said, you'd look fantastic. Listen, I could get you an appointment with Max. He's the guy who cut mine. I'll bet I could get you in someday this week after school. What do you say?"

Lori knew she had to think fast. "I may not have the money for a haircut this week," she offered hopefully. "I'll let you know. And anyway, tomorrow after school is out, I have to go by Pisano's and get something I forgot there." At least that part was true. She had forgotten to bring home the clothes that she had taken off and hidden behind the trash.

"Okay, but I'm telling you. It's what you ought to do. Catch you later."

"Bye," said Lori. Hildy had sounded disappointed, but that was all right. In this case, *stalling* was the name of the game. Stalling until she could avoid a punk haircut without losing Hildy for a friend.

Back in her room, she stood in front of her mirror trying to imagine how she would look with her long, dark hair cut short and spiked on top. Like I had stuck my finger in the proverbial light socket, she thought, and the idea made her giggle. And what on earth would Jody and Monica think?

Lori sank down at her desk and opened her Spanish book. She had tons of homework, but that was the last thing in the world she was in the mood to do. Irregular verbs. Yuk! She took a clean sheet of paper from her notebook, opened her Spanish book to the assigned page, and picked up her pencil. I'm all ready, she thought. Why can't I get started and get this boring stuff over with?

She gazed out her window. It had begun to snow, and in the glow from the street lamp she could see the lacy white flakes swirl and dance in the air. Her mind was swirling, too. Jody. Hildy. Monica. Tripp. Ed Beachley. The names were spinning around in her brain like snowflakes in a blizzard. She looked down, first at the pencil in her hand and then at the blank piece of paper, and she began to write.

Throwing Shadows

Who am I? I wonder, am I me?
And if not, who should I really be?
Was the way I felt yesterday the person I
   really am?
Or am I someone else, my past life a mere
   sham?

It's hard for me to know what others want
   of me.
And so I strive to become what they'd like
   me to be,
Casting my shadow on the ground. But
   instead of one,
There are shadows here, shadows there,
   shadows thrown all around.

Each one looks like me. But never, never
   could it be
The same as that which lies within. Each is
   far too fragile, far too thin.

For I am more than the shadows my friends
    see.
I am myself. I am me.

Without bothering to read it over, Lori folded
the paper and tucked it into the pocket at the
back of her notebook where she kept most of
her poems. She was exhausted, too exhausted
to think about irregular verbs. She changed into
her pajamas, slipped into bed, and was asleep
before she could say goodnight to Purr-vert.

Chapter 14

It had snowed all night, leaving a deep blanket of white over everything. Lori's spirits soared as she stepped into the clear, crisp air the next morning to walk to school. She felt better, as if her mood had changed to match the bright new look of the landscape. She always felt better once she wrote her feelings down on paper.

The first person Lori saw when she entered the school was Jody. She was standing beside the door to the office talking to a couple of other girls from the basketball team.

Jody looked up just as Lori walked past her. "Hi, Lori," she called. "How's the ankle?"

"Great," Lori answered. She joined the noisy crowd heading up the stairway and thought what a help her ankle had turned out to be. First, she had convinced Jody that she was a jock, too. Then when things had gotten to be more than Lori could handle, she had convinced Jody that she was an injured jock. Double faking, she thought and smiled to herself.

When she reached the second floor where the sophomore girls' lockers were located, she spotted Hildy and Candi coming toward her. Hildy ran toward her and pulled her aside as if she had something private to talk about.

"Has he called yet?" she asked in a loud whisper.

"Not yet," admitted Lori. "But it hasn't even been twenty-four hours since he talked to you." Somehow she couldn't imagine Ed Beachley needing extra time to get up his nerve, but at the same time, she didn't want to raise her expectations too high.

"Tonight. I bet it will be tonight," Hildy insisted. "Call me the minute you hang up from talking to him. Promise?"

"Promise," said Lori, holding up her right hand as if she were swearing a solemn oath. "You'll be the first to know."

With that assurance, Hildy swept on down the hall, and Lori looked after her, thinking how silly it had been to be depressed. She had super new friends and maybe, just maybe, the boyfriend of her dreams. She was having more fun now than anytime she could remember.

Monica was leaning against her locker when Lori sauntered up to it a moment later. "Hi, Lori," she said.

"Hi, Monica," Lori responded. She noticed that although Monica was smiling, she seemed a little sad. "What's up?"

"Not much," said Monica. "I called to see if we could walk to school together, but Stan said you'd already left. What took you so long?"

There she goes again, Lori thought, being possessive. "Nothing. Honest. I came straight to school," Lori said. "I'll bet it was that rat, Number Three. He probably just told you that. He's mad because I spent so much time on the phone last night."

Lori regretted the words the moment she spoke them. The two of them had *always* spent so much time talking on the phone. She hadn't meant to hurt Monica. A shadow passed over Monica's face for an instant and was gone.

"Gee, did you hear any good gossip?" she asked a little too brightly.

"No, not a thing," Lori mumbled. She turned toward her locker and started working the combination on her lock, feeling embarrassed. It had never been this hard to talk to Monica before.

Lori took off her down jacket and hung it in her locker. Did Monica really believe that everything was the same? Lori pulled out the books for her morning classes just as the first bell rang. Lori wondered how she could tell Monica that their friendship would have to be different. There wasn't any way to say it.

"So what have you been doing lately besides talking on the phone?" Monica asked as they headed for their classes.

Trapped again, thought Lori, but out loud she said, "Nothing much. Just hanging around." I can't tell you, Monnie! she thought.

They had reached the room where Monica had her first class, and she paused. "Want to walk home together after school? We can make some plans. There are a couple of good movies coming to Cedar Cinema Three this weekend."

"Sure," said Lori. They could talk then. She started to move on down the hall when she remembered her own after-school plans. "But I'm not going straight home. I have to go by Pisano's. I left something in the ladies' room."

Monica's eyes flashed. "When you said you'd just been hanging around, I didn't realize that you meant at Pisano's," she said, turning and marching into her classroom.

Well, what did she expect? Lori thought, her concern turning to anger. She dumped me for Steve. Was I supposed to turn into some kind of hermit? Still, she felt a little guilty. There had to be some way to let Monica know that she really was too possessive, and that she was missing a lot of fun.

The day remained relatively uneventful for Lori until classes changed between fourth and fifth periods. She came out of the classroom and glanced up the hall. Ed Beachley was heading her way. Her heart began pounding, and she prayed that she wouldn't blush even though her face already felt as though it were on fire. He was looking straight at her with that irresistible smile of his. Was this it? Was this when it was going to happen?

"Hey there, Lori," he called. "How's it going?"

"Great," was all she could say. He seemed to hesitate, and Lori thought for an instant that he was going to stop, but then he gave her a cocky grin and went on.

It doesn't matter, she thought. He noticed me. Maybe tonight he'll call.

After school, she headed for Pisano's, wondering briefly if she would see Ed there. A few kids hung out there after school, but mostly it was a weekend place. She was hurrying along, hoping that her clothes were safe, wondering if she should have called Papa Manetti to be sure, when she heard her name.

"Lori. Are you deaf? Wait up!"

She looked back over her shoulder. Tripp was crunching through the snow at a trot to catch up with her.

"Hi," she said. She was pleased to see him even if it had disturbed her to see him with Jillian Glenn at Pisano's. "What are you up to?"

"For one thing, I'm trying to catch up with you. I was going to call you tonight, but seeing you in person is better."

"Wow. I'm impressed," said Lori with a laugh. "And to what do I owe this sudden burst of popularity?"

"Your mind," he said. "Not that I'm not interested in your body. In fact, I plan to talk to you about that real soon, but at the moment it's your mind that I'm after."

"My mind?"

"Sure. You know you're always promising to show me some of your poetry. Well, now's the time. *Prisms* is coming out next Monday, and I have to have something of yours in it."

"No way," said Lori. "What I write is really private. I'd die if the whole world read it."

"Actually, our circulation isn't that big." Tripp

smiled broadly, and Lori smiled back. "Besides, you shouldn't be shy about letting people read your poems. Look at it this way. Writing is a form of communication, and you haven't really communicated if nobody ever reads what you've written."

"Tripp, when I write poetry I'm not really trying to communicate. I write it when I'm confused. You know, to try to sort things out. I can get in touch with myself better when I write. That's why my poems are so private."

"I see," Tripp said matter-of-factly. "And what you're trying to say is that you're some sort of freak of nature. And that no other kids ever get confused or need to sort things out. You're probably right. You probably don't have anything to say that would mean anything to other kids."

"Hey, wait a minute," Lori protested. Even though she knew he was teasing, she felt defensive. She would show him a thing or two. She opened her notebook and pulled out the poem that she had composed the night before. "Here, publish this one if you're determined to make me famous. But I want royalties!"

Tripp grabbed the paper and stuffed it into a manila envelope marked *Prisms*. "Thanks," he said. "And by the way, we pay in copies of the magazine." He trudged through the snow, leaving Lori to look after his retreating figure.

Had she just made a terrible mistake? It was true that lots of kids let Tripp print their poetry in *Prisms,* and most of it was just as personal as hers. Lori walked toward Pisano's, unable to shake her regret at having given her poem to Tripp. I'll call him tonight, she decided, and ask for it back.

Angela was tying a clean apron around her waist when Lori entered Pisano's. She seemed surprised to see Lori.

"Our pizza is so fabulous that you just can't stay away, huh?" Angela said, and smiled warmly. "How about a Coke on the house?"

"Thanks, Angela, but I probably shouldn't stay that long. I just came by to see if you found some clothes that I left in the ladies' room yesterday."

"If you're referring to a blue sweater, white long johns with a rosebud pattern, and a pair of yellow ski socks, you're in luck. But you'd better reconsider that free Coke. What are you going to do when you get home besides homework? Think it over while I get your stuff."

Angela disappeared into the Employees Only room, and Lori sat down at the counter, inhaling the delicious spicy aroma of pizza baking in the oven. She thought how great it would be if her own father could cook like Papa Manetti. Maybe I should have given him a gift certificate for pizza-making lessons for Christmas instead of a cookbook, she thought and then laughed aloud at the image of Stanley Byrum, Jr., Financial Consultant, tossing circles of dough into the air and catching them again the way Papa Manetti always did.

She was still smiling at that picture when she heard the door open. Before she could turn around to see who it was coming in, an arm slid around her shoulder, and a husky voice whispered in her ear, "Well, will you look who's here? If it isn't Lori Byrum, just the girl I wanted to talk to."

Ed Beachley. Lori's heart was pounding as she looked into his smiling face.

"Hi, Ed. Are you really looking for me?"

He slowly drew his arm from around her and straddled the stool next to hers, looking at her appraisingly. "Of course I'm looking for you. I've really been noticing you lately. I think we should get better acquainted. Don't you?"

Before Lori could answer, the door to the Employees Only room bumped open, and Angela backed out carrying a stack of clothing. "Here you are, Lori," she called without looking around. "Rosebud long johns and all."

Lori could feel the color rising in her face and hear snickering behind her. Ed spun around.

"Knock it off!" he ordered, and the snickering stopped. Turning back to her, he said, "You'll have to forgive those clods behind us. It's obvious that they have no class."

"Whoops!" said Angela. She lowered the things she was carrying out of sight beneath the counter and looked apologetically at Lori. "I'll get a bag for these," she said, and dashed out of the room again.

Lori sat there, not wanting to look right or left, wishing with all her heart that the floor would open up and swallow her. Still, Ed had come to her rescue and made the guys stop laughing. He had class, all right. She gave him a shy smile and relaxed a little.

Ed's finger brushed her cheek. "The reason I've been looking for you is to ask you to go out to a movie Friday night. What do you say? Are we on?"

Lori hesitated a moment, wanting more than anything to say yes. She was still embarrassed. Finally she smiled. "Well . . . okay."

Ed's eyes softened. "That's great. Look, Lori, I'll call you before Friday, and we'll decide what movie we want to see."

Angela had come back into the room carrying a large bag that said Pisano's Pizza across the front. She handed the bag to Lori.

"Thanks, Angela. I'd better get on home."

Lori said good-bye to Ed and made her way through the crowd of teenagers streaming into the restaurant. It was good to get out of there before someone decided to make another remark about her long underwear. She couldn't remember when she had felt so embarrassed, or so happy. She was actually going out with Ed Beachley on Friday night.

Chapter 15

True to her promise, Lori called Hildy as soon
as she got home from Pisano's. "It happened!
He asked me out for Friday night," she said the
moment Hildy said hello.

"Terrific! Tell me every word he said," begged
Hildy.

Lori filled her in on all the details, even the
story of the rosebud long johns. That brought a
howl from the other end of the line. "Listen,
Lori, this is the plan," Hildy said when she
finally stopped laughing. "I have a date with
Craig Jordon Friday night. I'll tell Craig that we
want to double. I know he'll go for it, too. He
and Ed are good friends."

"Super," said Lori. "Now all I have to do is
figure out what to wear."

"I'll have to admit that your wardrobe is the
pits," said Hildy. "But don't worry about that.
You've come to the right person. If I can't do
anything about your hair, at least I can do something about your clothes. We'll go shopping,

and I'll help you pick out something wild for your date with Ed. Which night can you meet me at the mall?"

"Gee, Hildy. I—"

"Don't argue," scolded Hildy. "Do you want to impress him, or don't you?"

"Of course I do, but—"

"Then which night can you meet me at the mall?"

"How about Thursday?" offered Lori.

"Thursday's great. What time?"

Lori thought for a moment. "Thursday is my night to do dishes, so how about right after school. That will give us a couple of hours."

The girls finished making their plans and hung up, and Lori paused for a moment and then picked up the phone again and dialed Monica's number. Even though their relationship was still strained, she just had to tell Monica about her date with Ed.

"Monica, you're not going to believe this," she said the instant Monica said hello.

"I'm not going to believe *what*!" cried Monica, catching the excitement in Lori's voice.

"Are you sitting down?"

"Of course not. How can I sit down when you say you've got news I won't believe? Come on. Tell me!"

"Okay. But you ought to sit down," teased Lori. "What is the greatest thing that could possibly happen to me?"

Monica groaned. "I don't know Lori. Are you going to tell me or not?"

"Ed Beachley asked me out for Friday night!"

"You're kidding. I don't believe it."

"See. I told you," said Lori. "It's true. You know I told you that I had to go by Pisano's after school. Well, he was there, and he asked me to go to a movie with him Friday night. Isn't that fantastic?"

Monica didn't say anything for a moment, and when she spoke again, Lori thought she detected a strange tone in her voice.

"Yeah, Lori. That's great news. I know how much you've wanted to go out with Ed. I'm glad he's finally noticed what a terrific person you are."

"Monica, what's wrong? You sound funny. Like you aren't really glad after all."

Monica was silent again, making Lori more puzzled than ever. Surely Monica didn't have a crush on Ed herself? Or was she jealous that Lori had a boyfriend? That had to be it. Monica would never stop being possessive.

"Lori, I don't know how to say this, but I don't think you should go out with Ed Beachley."

"What!" Lori yelled. "Why not?"

Monica sighed. "It's just that Steve told me some things about Ed."

"What things?" Lori demanded.

"Steve said that . . . well, that Ed's always bragging about what he gets from the girls he goes out with. You know. Naming names and telling details."

"Are you trying to say that he's some kind of sex maniac or something?"

"Something like that. Lori, you know I wouldn't

tell you that if I didn't think you ought to know for your own good."

Lori slammed down the receiver. Some friend. She can't stand a little competition, and then she has to try to spoil it when I finally get a date with Ed Beachley by saying awful things about him.

Lori fumed for the rest of the evening and was still angry at school the next day. She saw Monica in the halls a few times and glared at her. Monica looked hurt at first but then began returning the glares. All the other areas of her life were just about perfect. Jody continued to show concern for her ankle. Hildy assured her that everything was set with Craig for them to double on Friday night. And all Lori could think about was her date with Ed.

After school on Thursday, Lori rode the bus to the mall and hurried to the spot beside the escalator where she had agreed to meet Hildy. Hildy was already there. Her face lit up when she saw Lori making her way through the crowd, and she hurried toward her.

"I got here earlier, and I've found the perfect outfit for you," Hildy said, grabbing Lori by the arm and leading her down the concourse. "You're going to love it," she assured Lori. "But best of all, Ed's going to love it."

They turned into a small shop called Pizzazz that Lori had noticed often but had never been inside of. Their clothes were much more extreme than what she usually wore—with the exception of her one miniskirt. Leave it to Hildy to bring me here, she thought.

"I had the clerk put it aside for you," Hildy said. Then she waved to the clerk, pointed toward Lori, and before Lori quite knew what was happening, the clerk had thrust the outfit into her arms, and Hildy had pushed her into a dressing room. "Be sure to come out when you get it on so I can see how it looks," Hildy called in to her.

Lori looked at the outfit Hildy had chosen. It was a mind-boggling melange of orange and green neon. The knit shirt was white splashed with orange graffiti. The form-fitting leggings were orange also, but everything else was an electrifying shade of green. Hildy had thought of everything, from green leather ballet slippers and matching cotton socks to the bevy of green belts, accessorized with huge green earrings. One was the number one and the other was the number five. My age, she thought, and she couldn't help smiling.

"Are you dressed yet?" Hildy shouted through the crack in the dressing-room door.

"Hildy, you've got to be kidding. I can't wear this," Lori called back. "I'd feel like a clown."

"Don't be ridiculous. Just put it on. You're going to love it."

Lori shrugged and began changing into the neon clothes. When she had everything on, she stepped back and checked herself out in the mirror. What she saw surprised her. It's not really that bad, she thought. It's a little brighter than I usually go, but actually it's pretty cool. Her usually pale skin seemed to glow. The shirt and pants did not seem nearly so outlandish as they had on the hanger. They fit her well, accenting her best features, her extratrim waistline and long, slim legs. Maybe she shouldn't be so conservative. Maybe what she really needed was to brighten up a little.

Opening the door, Lori stepped out of the dressing room and walked over to where Hildy was pacing the floor.

"Is that fantastic, or is that *fantastic*!" Hildy shouted so loudly that several shoppers looked up and gave Lori approving nods. "Now you need a few bangles. Maybe a beret . . ."

"Hey, wait a minute," said Lori. "Don't get totally carried away. I can only afford so much. And, Hildy? Do you really think this looks okay on me?"

"Okay? Are you kidding? You look as if you should be jumping out of the pages of a fashion magazine."

The clerk was nodding in agreement. Another customer, a college girl, took an identical graffiti shirt off the rack and held it up in front of the mirror.

Lori was feeling more confident about the clothes Hildy had selected for her as she changed back into her old ones, but a new wave of depression swept over her as she totaled up the prices. Darn, she thought. I'm twelve dollars short of being able to get everything. She looked longingly at the number earrings. They were fourteen dollars. As much as she loved them, she would have to put them back.

"So what's the verdict?" Hildy demanded as Lori stepped up to the cash register.

Lori flushed. "I'm going to get them," she confessed. "Drab little Lori Byrum's coming out of her shell. I'm going to have to put the earrings back, though," she said sadly. "I just don't have enough money for everything."

Lori hung the earrings back on the display rack on the counter next to the cash register and watched the clerk ring up the sale. In the meantime, Hildy was acting so crazy, racing around the store slamming berets on her head and hanging wild sunglasses on her nose, that they were giggling wildly when they left the store and headed back out into the mall. As their laughter subsided, Hildy held up a fore-finger and said, "It's still early, and I have a terrific idea."

"What kind of idea?" asked Lori.

"I just thought up this terrific game that we can play. It's called 'fake shoplifting.' "

Lori frowned. "Fake shoplifting? What kind of game is that?"

"It's fake shoplifting," she repeated. "Like I've told you before, faking's the name of the game. All you do is watch to see that no clerks are looking. Then you pick up something and stash it in your handbag. Then you leave the store and walk around the mall. After a while, you go back into the store, make sure no one is look-ing, and put it back. It's as simple as that. There's no harm done. You don't really steal anything. It's just a fun way to test your nerve."

"Hildy, that's crazy. What if you get caught?"

"Don't be silly. Besides, like I said, we aren't going to really steal anything. It's only faking."

Then, seeing that Lori was still hesitant, she added, "Boy, Lori. You really are a child, aren't you? First it was TP-ing, and now it's this."

Hildy walked away, leaving Lori standing alone. Lori panicked for an instant. She didn't want Hildy to be mad at her. Maybe she should go along with the game. After all, she had never stolen anything in her life and didn't intend to. Since she wasn't going to steal, what could be the harm?

"Hildy! Wait up," she called. "I know that it's just a game, so I'll do it."

"Terrific!" said Hildy. "Sears is a good place because they're a big store and really busy. Their clerks never have enough time to watch for shoplifters." She took Lori by the arm and propelled her toward the entrance to the Sears store. "I'm going over to jewelry and check out the necklaces," she said once they were inside. "Why don't you head for the makeup. That stuff is easy to hide. I'll meet you back in the mall by the escalators in half an hour, and we'll compare our loot. And by the way, when you weren't looking, I dropped something into your bag from Pizzazz. It's nothing much. Just a little present I got for you in honor of your new image. Don't look at it until you get home. Promise?"

Hildy was gone before Lori could answer. She wondered briefly what sort of present Hildy had tucked into her bag, but right now she had work to do. A thrill of excitement traveled through her, and she hurried toward the makeup counter before she could lose her nerve. Being friends with Monica had never been this exciting.

The clerk behind the makeup counter was a middle-aged woman with dyed brown hair and long eyelashes, and Lori suspected that she used every item of makeup that she sold. The woman was busy putting streaks of foundation on a customer's hand, explaining as she went along about how one shade was too rosy and another too pale.

Lori inched closer to the counter. A shadow palette caught her eye. It contained at least a dozen colors, and she had wanted one like it for a long time. She fingered the palette and glanced toward the clerk again, raising only her eyes. The clerk was still busy, and a second customer was standing near, fidgeting impatiently. Hildy had been right. This was a busy store.

She glanced at nearby counters, but those clerks were busy, too. The timing was right. It was now or never. Keeping her eyes on the makeup clerk, Lori closed her hand over the palette and scooped it toward her, dropping it into her purse. Instinctively, she stayed where she was for a moment so that sudden movement would not be noticed. Then slowly she let out her breath and moved away.

She had done it. She had actually picked up something without anybody seeing it. She felt a terrific sense of exhilaration, as if she had a wonderful secret and was bursting to tell it. Smiling to herself, Lori turned away from the counter and then stopped cold. Tripp Lefcoe stood only a few feet away. One instant he was looking at her with a mixture of anger and disbelief, and the next he had turned and was stomping away through the crowd.

"Tripp!" she cried, but he did not stop. By the time she moved, he was out of sight, and she raced through the crowd frantically searching for him. I have to find him and make him understand, she thought. I just have to.

Tears spilled down her face as she raced from department to department, but there was no sign of Tripp. He had gone away, thinking she was a thief. Why had she let Hildy talk her into such a crazy thing in the first place?

Lori made her way back to the makeup counter where the last customer was paying for a purchase. The least she could do was pay for the eye-shadow palette, she decided. She had just enough money left. The clerk smiled warmly. "Have a nice evening," she said as she dropped the palette into a bag and handed it to Lori.

She nodded. She couldn't answer around the lump that was growing in her throat. How could she ever face Tripp again? Even if she explained, he might not believe her. As she drifted toward the mall, she became aware of commotion in another department.

Somehow Lori sensed what was happening before she turned and saw Hildy, wearing a horror-stricken expression, being led away from the jewelry department by a pair of security guards.

Chapter 16

Hildy was not at school the next day. Lori couldn't help feeling a little bit relieved, and a little worried. She dreaded facing her again. Especially since the "little present" that Hildy had slipped into her Pizzazz bag at the mall the night before had turned out to be the number earrings that Lori had wanted so badly but could not afford to buy for herself. She was sure that Hildy had not paid for them. Lori would have noticed if she had gone to the cash register after Lori put the earrings back. And Hildy couldn't have known ahead of time that Lori would not have been able to afford them. Fake shoplifting had been only too real.

Lori had slept very little. Part of the night had been spent thinking about Hildy. Lori wanted desperately to know what had happened to her after the security guards took her away. Surely they hadn't put her in jail. Hildy wasn't a bad person. She was just a little nutty sometimes. And she liked to show off. But of course the security guards would neither know about that nor care if they caught her stealing something.

And then there was Tripp. She couldn't get him out of her mind. The expression on his face was etched into her memory. How could she ever face him again? And how could she ever explain to him about Hildy's game of fake shoplifting? Except that Lori knew now that she had been foolish to believe it was a game.

Somehow she made it through the morning. She ducked every time she thought she saw Tripp in the halls between classes. She skipped lunch to avoid seeing him in the cafeteria. She decided to go for a walk instead.

Three blocks from Fairview was a small shopping center. Lori lingered there, looking in the shop windows but not really seeing the merchandise. She saw Tripp's face instead, and the hurt and confusion in his eyes. She thought about Hildy, too, and wondered why she wasn't in school. Passing a telephone booth, she paused. She could call Hildy and find out what was going on. At least that way she would know.

The phone rang six times before Hildy finally answered. "Franklin residence," she said softly.

"Hildy, this is Lori. Are you okay?"

"Yeah, I'm okay," she said, but Lori couldn't help thinking that she didn't sound okay. "I just didn't feel like seeing anybody today after what happened last night."

"What did happen?" asked Lori. "I saw you

with those two security guards, but they took you into the office and closed the door."

"They called the police! Even after I told them it was only a game and that I was going to put their crummy necklace back. You wouldn't have believed it, Lori. They treated me as if I were some sort of criminal."

Hildy was crying, and Lori tried to think of something comforting to say. She thought about just saying she was sorry, but somehow that sounded trite. Maybe I should just say exactly what I think, Lori mused. That I know it wasn't really a game. I owe her that much at least. But before Lori could respond, Hildy was talking again.

"The police took me to the station and called my parents, which was even worse," Hildy said. She was not crying so hard now, only sniffling softly now and then. "They were practically hysterical when they got there. My mom was crying, and my dad kept shouting about how he had let me off with a warning when I borrowed the car without asking, but that now he was going to get tough. So now I'm grounded for practically the rest of my life, and I have to go to court next Tuesday morning."

"Court?" Lori cried. "You actually have to go to court?"

"I told you they treated me like a criminal, didn't I? Dad called his lawyer this morning, though, and he said they usually just put you on probation if it's your first time. Can you believe this, Lori? Can you actually believe it? Anyway,

I'm not taking any chances on getting anything besides probation. I'm wearing everything purple that I own."

"Why purple?" Lori asked.

"Because I'm a Sagittarius, and purple is my cosmic color. It brings me luck."

Lori had to smile. In some ways, Hildy would never change. "I wish you a lot of luck, Hildy, and if I had anything purple, I'd loan it to you. I really would. I think that shoplifting last night was wrong whether it was fake or not. But I still like you a lot, and I think you're a good friend. Remember that, no matter what happens at court. Okay?"

"Sure," said Hildy, but there was uncertainty in her voice.

Lori took a deep breath and let it out slowly. "And about the number earrings, you know I love them and they are a super idea for a gift, but I'm going to take them back."

Hildy gasped. "Lori, you can't do that. They'll think you took them."

"No, they won't. I'll just tell them that the earrings must have slid off the counter and into my bag when the clerk was putting my things into it. Don't worry. I can handle it."

There was silence at the other end of the line for a moment before Hildy spoke. "Thanks," she said softly. "You really are a friend."

"I have to go now, Hildy. I'm calling from the shopping center near school, and it's almost time for the bell. I just wanted to make sure you were okay."

"I'm glad you called, Lori. Oh, and Lori, there's something I almost forgot. Now that I'm grounded, I won't be able to go out tonight." She paused a moment and then added wistfully, "Have fun with Ed."

Lori hung up the phone and headed back toward school, thinking how she had once felt as if she desperately needed Hildy's friendship and now it was Hildy who needed hers. In spite of all that had happened, Hildy's mention of her date with Ed made her tingle all over. It was really going to happen, and it would happen tonight. A vision flashed into her mind of herself, dressed in her fabulous new clothes, showing up at Pisano's after the movie with Ed Beachley. Everyone would be watching them. It would be the most exciting moment of her life. Still, Monica's warning kept nagging at her. What if Monica had been telling the truth? What if Ed really was a sex maniac? Now, with Hildy grounded, Lori would have to handle him alone.

By the time Lori started to dress for her date, her nervousness had escalated to pure panic. Purr-vert watched her solemnly as, with shaking hands she put on her graffiti shirt and orange pants.

"What are we going to talk about, Purr-vert? If I had trouble making conversation with Jody and Hildy, what on earth will I say to Ed Beachley? I just hope he doesn't want to spend the evening talking about the Duran Duran concert."

Lori finished dressing. Finally she eyed the

number earings lying on her dresser. They were the perfect finishing touch to her outfit. Maybe I can get a loan from my parents until I get another baby-sitting job, she thought. Then I could go out to Pizzazz, tell them the same story about the earrings falling into my bag by accident, and then pay for them. Lori held them up to her ears and inspected herself. No, she thought. Every time I wore them I would think of Hildy and shoplifting, and that would spoil the fun. Lori returned the earrings to her dresser and spun around.

"It's the new me, Purr-vert. How do you like it?"

Purr-vert blinked his big amber eyes a couple of times and then crossed the room, disappearing into the darkness of her closet.

Lori burst out laughing. "Thanks a lot," she said. "But you'll get used to it."

She was putting the last touches on her makeup when the doorbell rang at six-thirty sharp. She felt as though this evening would be the best one of her life. She took one last look in the mirror and headed down to meet Ed. She paused at the top of the stairs. Her father had answered the door, and the two of them stood just inside engaged in friendly conversation. Everything is perfect, she thought as she started down.

Suddenly from behind her came loud smooching noises, and at the same instant Ed looked up. Lori froze. Number Three! she thought. She wanted to race back upstairs and punch him out, but Ed was smiling up at her as if he hadn't heard anything at all. He looked so handsome that it took her breath away, and she went on down to meet him on wobbling legs.

"Hey, Lori. You look terrific," said Ed.

"Thanks, Ed. Good night, Dad," she said, and blew him a kiss. "We won't be late."

Lori grabbed her coat and hurried out the door before her father could say anything else. He had a strange look on his face when he saw what she was wearing. Semidisapproval, she thought.

Ed's sleek copper-colored Camaro sat in the driveway, and Lori slid into the bucket seat on the passenger side while he got behind the wheel. The engine roared to life, and he carefully backed the car out of the driveway and then zoomed off into the night.

Ed glanced at her with a grin on his face. "I just heard the news about you and Hildy lifting some stuff at the mall last night. Too bad that Hildy got caught." He moved his hand off the gearshift lever and gave her hand a squeeze. "But I'm glad you were smart enough not to."

"We weren't really going to keep those things," Lori protested, knowing that it wasn't entirely true but, at the same time, feeling disturbed at Ed's insinuation. "We just planned to walk around the mall with them for a while and then put them back. It was just a game that Hildy made up. She called it fake shoplifting."

"Sure. Sure. That's what they all say. Ask any guy in prison, and he'll tell you that he's innocent." Ed was chuckling and shaking his head. "I just think it's cool that you got away."

Lori didn't answer. She hadn't expected a thing like that from Ed. How could he think that anything about shoplifting was good. Tripp's face flashed into her mind again. *He* didn't think it was cool.

Ed pulled into the Cedarhurst Cinema Three parking lot and shut off the motor. He had said that she could decide which movie to see, and she stared at the marquee trying to make a decision. There was a horror movie, a war picture, and a love story. She had wanted to see *Love Letters* for a long time, but she knew that Ed would probably prefer anything to the love story.

"Why don't we see *Love Letters*," said Ed. "I'll bet you'd really like to see that one, wouldn't you?"

"Well . . . gee . . . Ed," Lori sputtered. "I'm sure you don't want to see something like that with two other good movies playing."

"Sure I do. Besides, I want you to have a really good time tonight."

He was looking at her with such a sincere smile that Lori wanted to freeze the moment in time. Monica was wrong. He really did care about her, after all.

The movie was sad, and Lori alternated between tears of sympathy for the poor heroine on the screen and intoxication from Ed's presence beside her and his arm draped tenderly around her shoulder. He moved closer and closer to her until she could hear his soft breathing and feel the warmth of his breath on her neck. Lori prayed that the minutes would pass slowly.

When "The End" flashed across the screen and the theater began to clear, Ed took her hand and drew her to her feet. "Let's get out of here," he whispered.

Back at the car, Lori sank back against the bucket seat, feeling as though she were drowning in happiness. They had been driving for several minutes and making conversation that seemed surprisingly easy when Lori suddenly realized that they were driving away from the bright lights of downtown.

"Where are we going?" she asked. "This isn't the way to Pisano's."

Ed gave her a cool smile, which looked almost like a leer in the harsh light of the dashboard. "We'll get to Pisano's later," he assured her. "In the meantime, we want to go someplace where we can be alone, don't we?"

Lori swallowed hard. She could feel a tingling on the back of her neck. "Sure, but . . . we don't want to miss seeing everybody."

"Relax," said Ed, and his hand found hers in the dark. "I just want to go someplace where we can talk. It's always crowded and noisy in Pisano's, and I want you for myself."

Lori's heart began pounding furiously. She wanted him to kiss her, but he was rushing things. If only Hildy wasn't grounded and she and Craig were in the backseat. Ed surely wouldn't try anything then. She hoped he would just kiss her. She could handle a kiss.

Ed pulled the car into a deserted lane, cut the lights, and pulled her toward him. "Rosebuds, eh?" he whispered hoarsely. Their lips met in the kiss she'd dreamed of for a year. His mouth was soft and sweet. Lori broke away, thinking that it had lasted too long. Ed yanked her close to him.

"Ed!" she shouted, and tried to pull away, but his grip was strong, and he would not let her go.

"Come on, baby. You know what I need. Thinking about you and those rosebuds is driving me crazy." His mouth came down on hers again, only this time it was hard and insistent. His hands moved up her spine.

Lori struggled and succeeded in breaking away from him. "Stop it, Ed! I mean it!"

Ed sighed and raised his arms in mock surrender. "Okay, kid, okay." He started the engine and backed the car out of the lane, heading toward town again. "We'll go to Pisano's if that's what will make you happy. Geez!"

They rode in silence. Lori could feel the flush of embarrassment on her face. Was he really coming on too strongly, or had she behaved like a prude? Maybe she had been too spooked by Monica's warning to behave in a rational way. Maybe I should apologize, she thought.

"Hey, Lori. I'm sorry," said Ed before she could speak. He was smiling and acting as if nothing had happened. As he pulled up in front of Pisano's he gestured toward the front door. "Here we are. Pisano's. Just like I promised."

Lori followed him into the crowded restaurant feeling more confused than ever. They found a booth in the corner, but Lori excused herself for the ladies' room. She said she wanted to repair her makeup, but really she needed to be alone to think.

The ladies' room was deserted, and she absently wiped away a lipstick smudge as she replayed the scene with Ed in her mind. He had behaved badly, just as Monica had said he would. But why had he suddenly apologized and insisted that they come here as if nothing had happened?

The door swung open, and she looked up to see Monica coming in. "Lori, I need to talk to you," she said. Then she added softly, "I'm here with Steve."

"Steve?" Lori said. "But what about Shana Beaumont?"

"I got to thinking about all that Steve had said. You know, about me being possessive and trying to run his life. I decided he was right, and I called him after school. I guess I've always been that way. Even when you and I went around together all the time," she added shyly. "I can see now that I shouldn't have been."

"Oh, Monica. We'll always be good friends," said Lori, putting her arms around Monica. "We've both learned that everybody needs a little space sometimes. I'm glad that you and Steve are back together."

"That's only part of what I came in here to tell you. I saw you come in with Ed, and I knew I had to talk to you right away."

Lori's heart skipped a beat. "And it has something to do with Ed?" she asked tentatively.

Monica nodded. "Steve knew that Ed asked you out for tonight, and he said that Ed told all the guys that he was going to show you a really good time because you could get him in to see Duran Duran."

Lori felt as though her heart would burst. Now she knew why he had insisted that they see the movie she wanted to see. And he had come on to her because that was just the kind of jerk that he was, but most of all it explained why he had suddenly become so apologetic and had brought her to Pisano's after all. Like he told all the guys, he wanted to make sure she had a good time. He didn't want to jeopardize his chances for getting to see Duran Duran.

"Well, I'll show him!" she said as anger erupted inside her. She stormed out of the ladies' room, ignoring greetings coming from several directions. She had one thing on her mind. Ed Beachley. At first she couldn't see him. He was not in the booth where she had left him. Then she spotted him leaning against the counter, wearing his usual cocky grin, and she marched up to him, fists on her hips.

"Have I got news for you," she said. He looked startled, but he didn't respond. A hush had fallen over Pisano's as she went on. "If you get in to see Duran Duran, it won't be because of me. And do you know why? I'll tell you why. I don't have a cousin on Duran Duran's crew. There is no Chris Byrum and there never was. I was faking it all along!"

Lori didn't wait for him to answer. She grabbed her coat from the abandoned booth and headed for the door. Suddenly she felt a hand close around her arm and she swung around angrily and then stopped. It was Tripp. He was smiling, and the look of hurt and confusion that had been in his eyes the night before had been replaced by confidence and pride.

"Come on," he said gently, "I'll take you home."

Chapter 17

Lori couldn't explain why she felt so fantastic when she climbed into Tripp's ancient Volkswagon bug. It coughed a few times before it started and finally bumped and jolted down the street.

"Tripp, about last night . . . " she began.

"You don't have to explain that," he said. "I think I'm beginning to understand what was going on. But I'll have to admit that you really had me going for a while." He was smiling again, and Lori thought her heart would burst with happiness.

"I thought I knew you," he went on, "knew what kind of person you were inside, but then you started doing so many things that were out of character that I decided I didn't know you after all."

"Things like jogging and eating yogurt?" Lori asked softly.

Tripp nodded. "Somehow you never came off as a jock before. Then I kept seeing you with Hildy, and that wasn't the you I thought I knew, either. I was just about to write you off as one more nut until last night."

"Last night?" Lori gasped. "But you were really angry with me last night. I could see it in your eyes."

"You bet I was angry. And hurt. I couldn't believe you would do something that stupid. But I saw you. I couldn't even talk to you then. I just left."

Swallowing hard, Lori asked, "Why can you talk to me now?"

Tripp didn't answer for a moment. Finally he said, "I read your poem again about throwing shadows, and then I realized that was what you had been doing. I also remembered that day in the cafeteria when you were asking about sports so you could talk to Jody Atterberry. I knew that you were trying to make new friends, but believe me, Lori, you were going about it all wrong. It was costing you more than you were getting back."

Lori smiled in the darkness, remembering for the first time that she had planned to ask Tripp to give the poem back. In the excitement of being asked out by Ed, it had completely slipped her mind. Now she was glad she had forgotten. Communication. That was what Tripp had said that writing was, and that if no one read what you wrote, you hadn't communicated. Tripp had read her poem, and now he understood who she really was. He not only understood, he approved.

"I was faking it," Lori said matter-of-factly.

"What a joke. At least now I know how dangerous that can be. I'm not really sorry that I did it.
For one thing, I learned that I'm not a jock and
never will be. Jody is a super person, but there's
no way that I can keep up with her and her
crowd."

Tripp laughed softly. "And Hildy?"

"This may sound funny, but Hildy needs more
friends, good friends anyway. I'm convinced that
she acts the way she does mostly to get attention. And I think Monica and I will be good
friends again, too, but in a different way."

They had reached the Byrum house, and
Tripp cut the lights and coasted to a stop in
front. Then he turned to her and tilted her
chin so that she looked into his eyes.

"I'm glad things are working out between you
and Monica," he said. "And the others, too. But
what about me? I care about you, Lori. I have
for a long time. I've wanted to ask you out, and
I probably would have if you hadn't seemed to
change. Like I said, I wrote you off and even
took Jillian Glenn out a few times, but I knew
right away that she wasn't the one for me. Then
I read your poem, and now I know that like the
poem said, you are more than the shadows your
friends see."

Lori felt her eyes grow moist in the warmth
of Tripp's tender gaze. Why had it taken her so
long to discover just how much he meant to
her? He had been here all along, she thought.
Sweet, sensitive Tripp.

"I think things are going to work out especially well between us," she said shyly.

Tripp pulled her close and kissed her, long and deeply. Her second sweet kiss that night, but this one was for real.

"I've got great news," her father said when she entered the kitchen the next morning. To Lori's utter amazement, he had *The Illustrated Step-By-Step Gourmet Cookbook* propped up on the counter, and he was surrounded by a large assortment of breakfast ingredients, bowls, spoons, and measuring cups.

Lori was still feeling the glow from Tripp's kiss. She smiled at his plunge into adventurous cooking. "Morning, Dad," she said. "What sort of good news?"

"You're not going to believe this, but I was able to get four tickets to Duran Duran. Four! The man who got them for me said it would take a miracle to get any at all, and then he came up with four. Isn't that great?"

Lori almost burst out laughing. Four tickets to Duran Duran were just about the last thing on earth that she wanted now. Still, she couldn't hurt her father's feelings after all the trouble he'd gone through to get them.

"Wow, Dad. That's terrific," she said. "Thanks a million."

"I suppose you'll invite that nice young man you went out with last night to use one of them. What was his name? Ed something-or-other, wasn't it?"

"Ed Beachley," Lori said. "No, I don't think Ed and I will be going out anymore." Then seeing her father's eyebrow shoot up, she added, "He's okay, but he's really not my type."

Who was her type, anyway? Lori wondered, as she opened the refrigerator to get the orange juice. Two weeks ago she wouldn't have known how to answer that question. Now she had a list.

Tripp was her type. She was his type, too. Monica was her type; she'd practically saved Lori's life last night by telling her the truth. And in time, with a little luck and some effort on both their parts, Hildy would be Lori's type. Not because they were alike but because they liked and respected each other.

Candi, Angela, Meg, and Trish—all of them were nice. Lori knew that on Monday morning she would be able to walk up to any of them and start a conversation.

But what about Jody? For an instant, Lori wondered if she should think of a story to tell Jody—how she'd suddenly decided to abandon athletics, as much as that meant to her.

No, Lori thought, getting a glass from the cupboard and pouring herself some juice. Tomorrow I'll go to the track and join her. I may not make it the entire five miles, but I'll go my own pace and explain that I'm just a beginner.

She vowed that after the run, she would suggest a restaurant that served both yogurt and hamburgers and fries. She smiled and realized that something delicious had started cooking a few feet away.

Hildy would have to understand that those Duran Duran tickets were for her to give to the friends she wanted to attend the concert with:

Monica, Steve, *Tripp*. Because Lori wasn't going to lie her way out of this one. Now, playing it straight was the name of the game.

At least, most of the time.